HIS ONLY NAME WAS WACO

A Texan who rode as an Arizona
Ranger, being peace-officer, detective
and ready to handle any emergency.
His duties led him to lock horns with
a campaigning lady politician; to
tangle with Curly Bill Brocious and
his girl-friend Tioga; to stand by
Captain Bertram H. Mosehan when
unscrupulous men sought to bring
about the disbanding of the Rangers.
In the end it led Waco to side with
Mosehan when the Ranger Captain
handled his most difficult and
dangerous task the only way he could
– by breaking the law himself. No
matter what he was called to do,
Waco did it and backed his play with
bold courage and a chain-lightning
fast draw.

WACO RIDES IN

CORGI BOOKS
A DIVISION OF TRANSWORLD PUBLISHERS LTD

WACO RIDES IN

A CORGI BOOK 0 552 08135 3

Originally published in Great Britain by
Brown Watson Ltd.

PRINTING HISTORY

Brown Watson edition published 1964
Corgi edition published 1969
Corgi edition reprinted 1972
Corgi edition reprinted 1976

PUBLISHER'S NOTE –
This book, while complete in itself, carries on the
adventures of Waco and Doc Leroy which began
in SAGEBRUSH SLEUTH and ARIZONA RANGER and precede
the happenings in the town of Two Forks described
in THE DRIFTER.

Corgi Books are published by Transworld Publishers Ltd.,
Century House, 61–63 Uxbridge Road,
Ealing, London W5 5SA
Made and printed in Great Britain by
Cox & Wyman Ltd., London, Reading and Fakenham

Waco Rides In

CHAPTER ONE

THE CAMPAIGNER

MRS BERTHA FORD stood by the window of the small hotel and looked down at Grant Street, Albion City, in Arizona Territory. The clock on the wall of her room showed eight o'clock on the final day of her visit. Down below, on the street, little stirred other than the dog which ambled along the rough, wheel-rutted surface until it came to a hitching rail post. Here the dog behaved as would any dog under the circumstances before ambling on out of sight. The street stayed still and deserted. Seated on the sidewalk facing the hotel, heads bowed as if sleeping, were two Apache bucks dressed in gaudy trade shirts, discarded army riding breeches and calf-high moccasins. The woman remembered seeing the same two braves seated in the same position just before she went to bed the previous night.

In her early forties Bertha Ford was a medium-sized woman with a good figure, red hair which even now only needed a little touching up to retain its colour, and a plain face. The eyes spoiled the face, they were cold and blue and seemed to be looking for the worst in everything or everybody they rested on. She wore a severe black dress, costly yet plain.

Her appearance gave no clue as to who she might be. She could have been a rancher's wife, or a mine owner's; she might have been the lady of some field rank army officer, even the madame of some better-class cat-house for such often dressed well yet severely and bore the same cold-eyed watchfulness.

In actual fact Bertha Ford was none of these. She was a political campaigner, hot and eager to see justice done to the down-trodden and the underdog.

To Bertha Ford anyone, Mexican, Apache or outlaw was down-trodden and the underdog if by being so they provided fuel to roast the Democrats who were in office.

Her stories about atrocities committed by the United States

Army against the Apaches had been gathered with some care. The fact she spoke neither Apache nor Spanish did not deter her. With a half-breed interpreter she scoured the reservations in Arizona Territory eagerly recording tales of brutality and outrage. The stories, telegraphed east as fast as they came to her, were pounced on and published by Republican or so-called independent newspapers of the less responsible kind and widely read. The same stories caused the Republican Party some embarrassment and lost them much support from their own voters or fence-sitters who might have gone their way in an election. The memory of Apache war, massacre and outrage still remained fresh in the public mind, for preceding Bertha's stories by a couple of weeks had been news that the Apache Kid and a band of bad-hat bucks ambushed and wiped out a cavalry patrol.

Bertha's stories raised a storm of protest and although the Republican Party stoutly affirmed she acted without their knowledge, they knew the damage had been done. One prominent Republican congressman, with a lifetime of politics behind him and a finger on the pulse of public support, said bitterly:

'After reading her stories I wish she'd start work for the Democrats.'

However, Bertha did not know how the Republicans regarded her and it is doubtful if she would have cared had she known. She did know there appeared to be a distinct chill amongst such influential Republicans as she met in Arizona Territory. She went on her way without troubling over this for her hatred rose beyond mere political differences.

The past three months in Arizona did not strike Bertha as being much success beyond her Apache stories. Her carefully gathered information about the exploitation and oppression of the Mexicans, told by an elegant Mexican lawyer who acted as her interpreter, attracted but little attention for the stories were never published. Only a month before Augustino Chacon and his *bandido* band struck a small hamlet on the border, leaving behind ten dead *gringo* men and three American women who wished death had struck them down before Chacon's gang laid hands on them. So little sympathy could be expected over the poor living conditions of the Mexicans and any newspaper foolish enough to try and raise sympathy would have speedily regretted it.

With much the same results Bertha, in desperation, tried to have published stories of brutalities committed by lawmen and prison guards against their prisoners. The belief that a criminal got what he deserved was widespread, and the few intellectuals who tried to establish a law-breaker as some privileged person to be pampered, given luxury and comfort while serving a sentence, as a warning not to do it again, found little support among the more sensible general public.

So on the last morning of her visit Bertha Ford felt she had achieved little. At half-past ten the stage would carry her on the first leg of the journey east. Her two previous trips, in the Kiowa country of Texas and the other amongst the Sioux, had been vastly more successful. Then, being unknown and un-suspected, she received co-operation and hospitality from the army. This time she received neither except when sheer neces-sity demanded it. Her stories came back over the telegraph wires as soon as they were published this trip, costing her the necessary cover of anonymity which shielded her on earlier tours. Without army aid she could do little and the army showed an understandable reluctance to help a woman whose aim was to smear them.

So Bertha stood by the window and allowed her niece to get on with the packing undisturbed. They had returned from an abortive visit to the San Ramos Apache reservation the pre-vious evening and soon would be attending a farewell break-fast engagement with several prominent Republicans who had gathered to see her leave – perhaps even to make sure she did leave.

The bored air left the woman. She tensed like a bird-dog hitting quail scent and leaned forward, pressing her nose against the window in her eagerness to take in every detail of the scene on the street below.

'Caroline,' she hissed. 'Come here, quickly!'

Caroline Banders left the bag she had just locked and joined her aunt by the window. She was a tall, slender, yet attractive blonde girl in her early twenties. Her face now bore a healthy tan, a rather fine drawn face, showing breeding and intelligence with a mouth which might smile easily in the right circum-stances. Her dove-grey travelling dress was neat without being fancy, ideal for riding in a stagecoach.

'What is it, Aunt Bertha?' she asked.

'Look!' Bertha replied, gripping Caroline's arm and point-ing.

They travelled slowly, the three men in the lead staggering, their clothes shedding dust at every step. They walked with dragging feet, heads hanging in exhaustion, like men driven

9

beyond human endurance. The two at the front stumbled awkwardly side by side, close together, but not for mutual support. From one's right wrist to the other's left hung something which glinted in the rays of the morning sun. They were handcuffed together. The third man stumbled blindly along behind the two. His wrists had no handcuffs and needed none for his right arm hung in a rough sling. Yet his lack of a gunbelt and the dejected way in which he walked showed he was as much a prisoner as the other two.

The fourth of the party might be tired but he walked as a free man. In height he stood over six foot, a wide shouldered, lean waisted young man. The expensive black J.B. Stetson hat's true colour lay almost hidden under a coat of dust but like any true Stetson held its shape. It was a Texan's hat, the broad brim, the low crown's shape and the way of wearing telling that to western eyes. The hat, like all his clothes, spelled cowhand from Texas. The shirt, levis, fancy stitched boots with the ever attached Kelly spurs bore a coating of dust, the shirt and levis grimy and dirt-streaked under the dust. The face, whiskerbristled and dirty, still looked young, could have been handsome, strong and virile when clean. The eyes were the blue of a June sky after a storm, firm, strong eyes which might have been happy and friendly, although were not at that moment.

The cleanest thing about the young man was the brown leather buscadero gun-belt with the matched, staghorn butted Colt Artillery Peacemakers in the holsters. The holsters were of a kind not one man in a hundred wore – or could make best use of. They fitted the contours of the guns, leaving half of the chamber and all the trigger guard exposed for speedy removal. The gun-belt, like the clothes, told a story for such a rig meant its owner could draw, shoot and hit his mark in less than a second. That kind of man always kept his guns and rig clean.

Following the men came a huge paint stallion, moving without needing to be led by the reins and looking as leg weary as the men. Its low horned, double girthed Texas saddle carried nothing more than five gun-belts which looped around the horn, a coiled Comanche hair rope, a bulky set of saddlebags behind the cantle. A new model Winchester Centennial Model of 1876 rifle showed its butt from the saddleboot under the left stirrup.

The men walked slowly along the street, heading for the sheriff's office farther down it. The tall Texan must be taking his prisoners to the cells behind the office.

'I must look into this,' hissed Bertha Ford, twisting her head to watch the procession as far as she could.

'Must you?' replied the niece.

Never a woman sensitive to atmosphere Bertha did not notice the bitter note which came into her niece's voice.

Looking at the wall clock Bertha clucked her tongue in annoyance. 'The stage leaves at half-past ten and I've that breakfast engagement to keep. There might be a chance of my going down after it's over. There's a story in it, I'm sure. I wonder who that brute worked for, I could see no sign of a badge.'

'He might be a bounty hunter,' Caroline remarked.

'That's possible, I suppose, but I doubt it.'

Bertha Ford did not want to believe the man was a bounty hunter. Such men only rarely worked for official law enforcement bodies and so offered little which might be turned into anti-Democrat material. She tried to see if any further development might justify her cancelling the breakfast engagement but the men were out of sight and she turned from the window.

'Let's go downstairs, dear,' she said. 'I might find time to investigate this business later.'

Two men stepped from the door of the Albion City sheriff's office to stand side by side on the sidewalk, hands thumb-hooked into their belts.

Both were lawmen, the smaller wearing the badge of county sheriff. The other showed no badge but was no less a lawman because of the omission. A tall, wide shouldered, powerful man approaching his fortieth year without an ounce of fat to mar his frame and without more than a hint of grey in his brown hair. His moustache was neatly trimmed, framing a mouth which was firm yet had the saving grace of humour. His clothes were of the style a prosperous rancher wore, his gun-belt, with its low-tied, ivory-butted Colt Cavalry Peacemaker, a fast man's rig. In appearance he could have been a tough, practical rancher, a man who spent much time in the saddle and never gave an order he could not obey himself. In a sense the appearance did not lie. He'd been superintendent of the great Hashknife outfit but no longer held that post. His name was Bertram H. Mosehan and his official title Captain of Arizona Rangers.

Mosehan and Sheriff Caudell stood on the sidewalk for a moment without speaking. Opposite the office, before the Wells

Fargo depot, sat a pair of Apaches, apparently asleep. Caudell indicated them with a jerk of the thumb.

'Still here,' he said. 'It looks as if your report was right after all.'

'My reports mostly are,' replied Mosehan. He was a man like that. If a thing needed to be said he said it without flinching or avoiding the blunt issues. 'None of my boys have made it here yet.'

'You couldn't expect any of them to, not in the time they've had.'

Mosehan grunted, a grunt which might mean anything. He might, and often did, excuse any action his men made in the execution of their duty. He would not allow anyone, even a friend of long standing like Caudell, make excuses for the men in their absence.

'I'll have to telegraph the Governor and tell him I can't make the conference,' he said, more to himself than to Caudell. 'If none of the boys make it I'll have to cover the coach myself. It's got to be done.'

Caudell agreed with Mosehan. His eyes flickered to the front of the Wells Fargo office, deserted and empty at this hour although from behind came the sounds which told of a team being prepared to take the ten-thirty east-bound stage on its run. The situation was dangerous, the report Mosehan received needed attention.

With that thought in his head Caudell glanced up the street. He gave a low startled curse, caught Mosehan's arm and tugged at it.

'Hell fire, Bert. Look along there.'

Mosehan turned. His eyesight was every bit as good as the sheriff's and he studied the approaching men. Something like relief came to Mosehan's expressionless face as he recognized the tall young Texan who walked behind the others.

The sheriff felt no relief, only the cold sweat of anxiety. The county elections were close and he knew how delicate was the balance on which his position hung. He knew who stayed at the hotel the previous evening. If *she* saw the procession she would be at the jail, demanding answers, preparing a report which might even end in Washington for investigation.

The three staggering prisoners turned blindly towards the jail, moving like men in a trance. One of the handcuffed pair stumbled but the other made no attempt to help him, only tugged at the connecting links and weakly mounted to the sidewalk. The other man caught his balance with an effort and followed. The last and youngest of the trio followed them, a sob of relief and exhaustion breaking from his lips as he reeled past the sheriff and through the door.

Caudell followed the prisoners into the office. His two deputies and Mosehan's young clerk came to their feet as the men staggered in. Caudell snapped an order for his deputies to see the prisoners into a cell, then fetch a doctor. Jed Franks, the clerk, walked through the door and towards his boss.

The young Texan leaned on the hitching rail and looked with tired, dull eyes at Mosehan.

'Howdy, Cap'n Bert,' he greeted. 'I never thought to see you here.'

'The Dansfield bank bunch, boy?' Mosehan said gently.

'Yep.'

'Were five of them, way I heard it.'

The Texan waved a grimy hand towards his horse 'There's five gunbelts and the money on my kak.'

Mosehan stepped from the sidewalk and walked towards the big paint, keeping a wary eye on it. He lifted the bulky saddlebags from the cantle, then removed the gunbelts from the horn, noticing the rusty coloured smear across the leather and buckle of one belt. He did not need to ask what the smear had been caused by.

'Go into the office and rest, boy,' Mosehan ordered. 'You look like you've been missing some sleep.'

'Some. I'll tend to this ole Dusty hoss of mine first.'

'I'll do it for you,' Jed Franks offered. 'Go and rest, Waco.'

The young Texan whose only name was Waco shook his head, the grin on his face more like the grimace of a sun-bleached skull. His paint stallion might be leg-weary but would still not allow just anyone to handle it, even a man who'd been around as much as the young clerk. The paint tolerated few people. Jed Franks, for all his working for the chief of the Rangers, did not have the horse-savvy to tend the paint without winding up on the ground, wearing its shoes for a teeth brace.

'Come on,' said Waco, his Texan drawl holding a friendly note. 'I'll let you tote the saddle back from the civic pound.'

Mosehan opened his mouth and closed it again. His business in Albion City was important, the kind of chore only one of his Rangers might handle. He had scattered telegraph messages to towns where some of his Rangers might find them and know he needed help in Albion, but without results. Now Waco had arrived but did not look in any condition to handle the chore.

In this Mosehan cast no reflection on Waco's abilities at other times. He stood fully capable of handling any duty, no matter how dangerous or important, that an Arizona Ranger might be called on to do.

An orphan almost from birth, Waco had been raised on a Texas ranch and at thirteen never rode without a Navy Colt by his side. Two years later he worked for Clay Allison and neither man nor boy rode for the Washita curly wolf's brand unless he could handle a gun. Waco could handle one. In fact he'd been well on the way to becoming another Bad Bill Longley or John Wesley Hardin, a hunted killer with a price on his head. Then he fell in with the Rio Hondo gun-wizard, Dusty Fog, and his life was changed. Dusty Fog had saved Waco's life at some risk to his own.* Then he took the proddy youngster under his wing, changed him from a potential killer to a useful member of rangeland society. First as a cowhand working on the OD Connected as a member of Ole Devil Hardin's floating outfit, later as a deputy town marshal in Mulrooney, Kansas,† Waco learned his trade, learned it well. Each member of the floating outfit taught the youngster something and he proved to be an apt pupil in every subject. He learned to use his fists and handle himself in a rough-house brawl, to read sign where a buck Apache might falter. He knew the tricks and ways of crooked gamblers, most he knew *when* as well as how to handle his guns. From Dusty Fog he learned the most. To use his eyes, his brains and knowledge to probe into the motives and actions of men. The knowledge served him well as an Arizona Ranger.

Waco did not come to Arizona with the intention of joining the Rangers. He caught a bullet helping the other members of the floating outfit handle a dangerous situation.‡ The wound took longer to heal than was expected and the others, with the exception of Doc Leroy, headed back for Texas. Then on their way home Waco and Doc took on as round-up hands at the Hashknife outfit. This was a temporary measure, to refill their depleted wallets. Captain Mosehan saw the way Waco and Doc pitched in on some rustler trouble and asked them to come with him when the Governor of the Arizona Territory asked him to form the Rangers. Mosehan never found cause to regret his choice of men and for the past two years they'd done much to help smash the lawlessness of the territory.§

* Told in TRIGGER FAST.
† Told in THE TROUBLE BUSTERS and THE MAKING OF A LAWMAN.
‡ Told in RETURN TO BACKSIGHT.
§ Told in SAGEBRUSH SLEUTH and ARIZONA RANGER.

14

After attending to his horse Waco headed for the jail with Jed Franks carrying his saddle and asking eager questions that did not receive any answer. Waco entered the jail and sat at the desk, resting his head on his hands. Mosehan looked down at the young Texan and wondered if he might possibly be in any shape to handle the important task.

Caudell came into the office and dropped a pair of hand-cuffs on the table by Waco's elbow.

'Did you have to bring them in like that?' he asked.

'They wouldn't have it any other way,' Waco replied.

'I mean like *that*—on foot and—'

'Mister,' growled Waco, lifting his face to look with sleep dulled eyes at the sheriff. 'They robbed a bank. Left three harmless folks dead in it. They left one of *your* deputies laying in the street with his brains on his face and no back to his head. I went after them alone because there wasn't time or the men on hand to form a posse. Those five run their hosses until they started dropping under 'em. First they rode double, then three on one hoss, two on the other. When I caught up they were all trying to fork the one remaining hoss. It got loose and high-tailed in the fuss that followed. What the hell should I have done?' He paused, cold eyes never leaving Caudell's face. 'Set the three on the back of my old Dusty hoss and lead them in?'

Mosehan laid a hand on Waco's shoulder and pressed gently. 'Ease off, boy. You didn't pick the best time to come in.'

'You sure didn't,' agreed Caudell fervently. 'With *her* at the hotel.'

'She doesn't come into it,' barked Mosehan. 'The boy brought in three prisoners the only way he could and I'd face down the devil himself afore I'd let him call one of my men down for doing his duty.'

Mosehan was sincere in his words. His organization owed no allegiance to the political factions of the Territory. Some might be stout Republicans, others equally firm for the Demo-crat cause but they forgot such things when taking the oath as Arizona Rangers. Mosehan's words explained why the Rangers were such a loyal and tight-knit group, ready and willing to light down in hell and haul a shuck out of it in the face of the devil if Mosehan gave the word. They knew their leader stood behind them and would back every action, any method used in the execution of their duty, regardless of the consequences.

'What I mean is the boy's first to reach Albion,' Mosehan finished.

Sheriff and Ranger Captain exchanged glances. Then Caudell

looked down at Waco who appeared to be almost falling asleep as he sat at the desk.

'You can't send him out on that chore, Bert.'

'What chore's that, Cap'n Bert?' Waco inquired.

'It's an urgent one, boy. Real important.'

'When do I start?'

There spoke the spirit of the Arizona Rangers, not asking what dangers the job might entail or even what the job was. Just one simple thing need be settled. 'When do I start.'

'There's a bath-house at the back of the barber's shop,' Mosehan replied. 'Let's go down there. You can shave, get some of that dirt off, some clean clothes on and we can talk while you're doing it.'

Reaching down Mosehan opened the desk cupboard and pulled out a tarp-wrapped bedroll. On his way to Prescott for a conference called by the Governor, Mosehan's route took him through the small town of Dansfield. There he heard of the bank robbery and that one of his men had taken out after the gang. From the description Mosehan knew the man to be Waco and discovered the young Texan had left his bedroll in town to travel lighter. Knowing Waco would return any of the outlaws he might take to Albion, the county seat, instead of Dansfield which possessed no facilities for holding dangerous prisoners, Mosehan brought the bedroll along. Now Mosehan felt pleased he had done so for this other business came up and Waco would need the contents of his warbag which lay in the roll.

'There's a clean shirt, underwear, socks and a bandana in my warbag,' Waco remarked, coming to his feet. 'You'll have to stand me a new pair of pants, I'm near on broke.'

Mosehan grinned, opening the tarp, unrolling the suggans and blankets and taking out the warbag. He slung it on to his shoulder, gave Franks an order to make for the nearest store and buy some pants, then went with Waco towards the barber's shop.

The owner of the business house that ran the baths, being one of the many people who regarded the Arizona Rangers with some esteem, was more than willing to bring hot water and fresh towels. He waited until Waco stripped off the dirty clothing then took up the boots and hat promising they'd be returned better than new by the time he was done with his bath.

Mosehan drew up a chair, watching Waco's muscular young frame sink into the hot water to the accompaniment of a delighted gasp as the heat bit into him.

'The stage leaves at half-past ten, boy. I want you on it.'

'I'll make it,' promised Waco.

'You likely saw the Apaches sitting around on the way in?'

'Why sure. Chiracahaus from the San Ramos reservation, I'd say. Which same I've been through Albion three times and seen Apaches every single time.'

'Yeah, Apaches aren't anything unusual here,' Mosehan drawled. 'Only we're likely to see more of them than we want unless you find out what's needed on that stage today. Just start in to using that fancy dude soap, it'll make you smell nice in the company.'

Waco grinned then began to lather his arms. The grin died as he caught the meaning of the words. Waco had seen Apache war when, with Dusty Fog, he helped defend the town of Baptist's Hollow from the warrior horde of Lobo Colorado.* Yet the San Ramos reservation never gave trouble, for the man who ran it knew Apaches and dealt fairly with them.

'I don't get you, Cap'n Bert.'

'Did you ever hear about Mangus Colorado's medicine?'

'Why sure. 'Bout as much as any white man has. It's hid out under guard on the San Ramos reservation some place, isn't it?'

'It *was* hid there some place.'

'You mean it's gone?' asked Waco, sitting up erect.

'That's just what I mean. One out of six people could have taken it and all six are on the stage this morning.'

'What was it they, or he, took?'

'Like I said,' Mosehan replied. 'Mangus Colorado's medicine but what that is I don't know. The man who told me doesn't know. He's a squaw-man, lived with the Chiracahaus most all his grown life but he's still white and they've never let him see the medicine. I'm certain he didn't take it, so that leaves the six on the stage.'

'Who are they?'

'Cody Yarrow, he's one of Sieber's Apache Scouts. Going on furlough and was on the reservation seeing some friends. He knows Apache and speaks their language, could know where the medicine was hid. Frank Wilson, gambler, tinhorn or I miss my guess. Was out at the San Ramos fort, used to go riding each morning on the reservation and played poker, or took money from the soldiers at night. Julie Clover, a pretty fair singer. Went out to the fort to sing in the sutler's place. The Reverend Samuel Hodges, he's been on the reservation for

* Told in APACHE RAMPAGE.

17

a month, trying to convert the Apaches, pulled out sudden, like all the others. Then there's Mrs. Bertha Ford and her niece. You know who she is?'

'I know,' agreed Waco. 'Read one of her stories in the *Prescott News Herald. "Is your son a legalized killer?"* it was called. All about how a bunch of peaceful Apaches got themselves wiped out by cavalry, artillery and Gatling guns at Baptist's Hollow when they came in to church. Lord, I was never so sickened in all my life.'

'I've seen some of her stuff,' Mosehan replied. 'But don't sell her short, boy. She's got some influence back east. She could still be the one, a trip like the one she's just finished costs plenty and she might need the money. A thing like Mangus Colorado's medicine'd bring in good money from some eastern collector or tent showman.'

'Haul them in and search them,' suggested Waco.

'You reckon I'd've passed that one up, happen I thought it would help?' the Ranger Captain grunted. 'We don't know for sure what we're after. There's no word leaked out about this so far and happen we start searching there'll be questions asked. If folks heard they'd start screaming for the cavalry to move in and that'd bring things to the boiling point all right.'

Waco ducked his head under the water, came up and began to soap his blond hair. He thought over what Mosehan told him so far and saw the wisdom in the words. He knew how quickly people spooked when they thought Apache trouble about to start. Indian-fever, fear of attack, loomed large in the thoughts of any town near to an Apache reservation. If once word got out that the Apaches had lost an article of value to them, some fool would start screaming that the army did something. In a tense situation such as this one spark might cause an explosion and the braves take out in a full-scale uprising. Then the other badhats would put on the paint and once more the bitter, bloody struggle to subdue the Apaches fall upon the land.

Ducking his head under the water Waco washed the suds from his hair and looked at his boss on emerging.

'So you want me on the stage, learning what I can and seeing if I can get back the medicine?'

'Sure,' agreed Mosehan.

'It might not be one of them.'

'It might not. But I reckon the Apaches have a better than fair idea who's got it. I made the rounds with Brick Caudell last night and saw their scouts. They covered two hotels and the livery barns. Thing is the passengers of the stage were all in one or the other hotel the Apaches watched.'

'Looks like you're right – for once.'

Mosehan grinned. 'You've three days to the New Mexico line. I want the medicine finding and fetching back before they cross the line. I'd don't reckon any of them know you.'

'Cody Yarrow might,' Waco answered. 'But he won't let on who I am.'

'He's a suspect, boy. Might be the one who took it. You'll have to go real careful all the time.'

'Aren't I always?' grinned Waco.

'Nope!'

'Couldn't you talk with the chief of the reservation, find out what we're after?' Waco inquired.

'If I could I'd be out there doing it now. You know how close-mouthed they get about their religion.'

'I know.'

'You're not going to get much sleep, boy. If you get any afore the stage pulls out.'

'I'll get some on it,' drawled Waco finishing his bath and climbing out to take the towel Mosehan offered. 'I likely won't do anything afore we hit Ma Randle's place tonight.'

Jed Franks entered at that moment with four pairs of levis trousers over his arm. 'I didn't know your size, *amigo*,' he said with a grin. 'So the storekeeper told me to bring these and let you pick the right ones.'

Mosehan accepted the trousers and asked Franks to make for the jail to arrange a meal to be ready when Waco returned from his bath. Waco selected the best fitting trousers and pulled them on over his underpants. He turned back the cuffs in the approved cowhand style then straightened up and prepared to shave the three day growth of whiskers from his face.

Waco looked, even if he did not feel, refreshed and alert when he walked into the sheriff's office and sat at the desk to eat the meal which Jed Franks brought in. The young clerk knew the gravity of the situation and showed he knew what a man might need to handle it. The gunbelt lay on the desk and Jed opened a box of .45 bullets to refill the empty loops. Waco, his mouth full of eggs and bacon, nodded his thanks. The stetson on the table and Waco's boots showed the owner of the bath-house kept his promise. That hat looked like new and the boots bore a shine reserved for special occasions when Waco himself had the shining to do.

While Waco sat eating he saw the stage brought around to the front of the office, pulled by two horses and left ready for the heavy baggage to be loaded on top and the regular team harnessed. The driver climbed on top and started to load the bags thrown to him by the guard.

'Take care of my rifle and ole Dusty hoss,' Waco said to Mosehan, pulling his plate to one side and getting to his feet, 'Where'd you want me to report in?'

'Catch the first stage back here,' Mosehan replied. 'I'll leave that paint crowbait in the civic pound. Here's your stageline ticket, don't lose it.'

'I'll surely try not to, pappy,' drawled Waco, sounding like a son answering his doting and worrying parent. 'Reckon I'll head across their right now.'

'The stage don't leave for almost an hour,' Mosehan pointed out.

'Which same's why I'm going now. I can get some sleep afore it starts.'

Waco took up his bedroll, re-wrapped ready for him, the box of bullets put inside by Jed who did the rolling. Mosehan handed Waco his rifle remarking he' would leave the saddle on the sheriff's burro out back. The young Texan nodded, slung the bedroll across his shoulder, looked at the rifle and tossed it to Mosehan.

'I'm not likely to need it,' he remarked and walked from the room.

'Is he as good as I've heard?' Caudell inquired, watching Waco stride to the stagecoach.

'He's likely the best man I've got, up to and including my sergeant,' Mosehan replied. 'And if any man can get back the medicine he'll do it.'

The driver caught Waco's bedroll, opened his mouth to growl an angry comment, saw the tired look about the young Texan and closed his mouth again. After a hard night's celebration in a saloon the driver felt in an irascible mood but he was cautious with it. He did not know who Waco might be, but knew full well *what* he was.

The same irascible mood had led the driver to place his coach right close to the hitching rail so his passengers would be forced to walk around into the street before they could enter. Waco found some satisfaction in the arrangement for it meant he could take a corner seat and remain undisturbed by people pushing past him as they entered. So Waco took a seat with his back to the team and at the far side against the window.

He settled down, drew his hat over his eyes and went to sleep.

Mosehan crossed the street with a package of food Waco had forgotten but the Texan was asleep before he reached the coach so he passed it up to the driver who accepted it with an eagerness at odds with his sullen behaviour earlier.

'He one of your boys, Capn?'

'He sure is,' agreed Mosehan. 'You stay where you are, friend, and let him sleep his sleep.'

The driver grinned. He'd placed his coach in this position out of sheer orneriness but it looked as if the head of the Arizona Rangers approved his actions.

The passengers for the east bound coach gathered before the Wells Fargo office and watched their over-night bags placed in the rear boot, then lashed into place ready to roll.

Cody Yarrow had been first to arrive, a tall, wide shouldered young man in the buckskin shirt, cavalry trousers and moccasins of Sieber's Apache Scouts. Around his waist the gunbelt was of military pattern, the walnut handle Cavalry Peacemaker riding butt forward at the left while a staghorn handled bowie knife hung sheathed at the right. He tossed his bag to the driver and stood watching the other passengers come up.

Next to come, dressed in sober black suit, white shirt and cravat, was a sallow faced, gaunt man of indeterminate age. He wore the round topped black hat of a frontier circuit riding preacher and held a thick, leather-bound bible in his left hand. Even at this early hour of the morning sweat trickled down his face and he did not speak as he handed his bag to the driver.

A young woman and a gambler walked towards the coach side by side. The woman stood at most five foot two and wore a small hat with a feather in it on her piled up rusty-coloured hair. Her face had a certain attractive charm, and her dark blue satin dress revealed a shapely figure of the plump, eye-catching kind which was the current style among theatricals. In her right hand she carried a vanity bag, in the left a parasol, neither of which could a lady of her class be seen without.

The gambler's face had a pallor through which the dull blue of his facial hair showed. In height he stood only six inches taller than the woman, but was stocky and hard looking. The butt of a Merwin & Hulbert pocket revolver showed from a shoulder clip under his coat. His shirt, frilly fronted, silk, and looked expensive while his trousers were tight legged and stylish. He gave his bag to the driver, growling out an angry inquiry why the stage came to be left in such a position.

'Happen you don't like it, mister, find some other stage, snapped the driver, bad temper regained. 'This'n stays where she be.'

The gambler opened his mouth to make a reply then closed it again as he saw Bertha Ford and her niece approaching. He looked them both over with a casual yet calculating glance and could have guessed to a dollar how much every stitch of clothing cost. He fancied himself as a student of such matters and knew the two women had money, enough to make it worth his while to cultivate them. The girl was a better than a fair looker. He had spent time with worse looking if they were wealthy and unattached.

'Let's get 'em aboard,' the driver called as he took the remaining bags. 'I'm pulling out in five minutes ready or not.'

Cody Yarrow pulled open the door, glanced inside at the sleeping form of Waco, then held out his hand to help Caroline climb in. 'Was I you I'd take the side seat facing that sleeping gent, ma'am,' he said, his voice a sleepy Texas drawl. 'It'll be easier riding for you.'

Caroline nodded her thanks. Her cheeks flushed with pleasure for many weeks had gone by since last a young and presentable man addressed her in such a manner. She took the advice and sat facing Waco; her aunt followed her and took the seat by her side. Bertha threw a look at Waco's sleeping form trying to decide where she had seen him before. The rusty-haired young woman entered and sat next to Waco, ignoring the disapproving glance Bertha threw in her direction. The gambler came next, sitting by the young woman, the black-dressed man taking the window seat by his side and Cody Yarrow occupying the remaining place.

Just as the driver climbed aboard the Wells Fargo agent came dashing from his office, a thick, bulky envelope in his hand. He leaned across the hitching rail and looked in the window towards Caroline.

'You Miss Banders, ma'am?' he asked.

'I am,' she agreed, holding out her hand. 'I thought this might catch up with me here.'

The agent handed over the letter and jerked back as with a yell and a whip crack the driver started his team moving. The coach lurched once before settling down to rock back and forwards on its springs. Caroline caught her balance and thrust the envelope into the vanity bag she nursed on her knees.

'Who is that from, dear?' asked her aunt.

'It's material for my book,' Caroline replied, turning to look at the town as it fell behind them.

Once again Bertha opened her mouth to ask more questions, then closed it. A public discussion of family affairs was not desirable, especially in front of the sort of people the other passengers appeared to be. So she sat back in the seat and thought of the good story she had been forced to leave behind. Her hosts at the breakfast engagement showed little interest in the story of the lawman herding prisoners like cattle. More, they appeared to change the subject every time she made an attempt to bring it up. It almost seemed that they did not want her to investigate the matter.

The rusty-haired young woman looked her fellow passengers over with the easy familiarity of one who entertained people for a living. 'We've got a lot of miles to cover,' she said in a friendly tone, 'Might as well know what we can call each other. I'm Julie Clover.'

'Cody Yarrow, on furlough from the Apache Scouts. I heard you sing one time in Tombstone, Miss Julie. Right purty it was.'

' "Thank you, kind sir," she said,' laughed Julie.

'I'm Frank Wilson,' the gambler put in, speaking directly to Caroline. Then his eyes went to Cody, seeing a possible rival for the girl's attention. 'I've heard tell of you, Yarrow. They reckon you're a knife-fighter. Never took to knife-fighting nor fighters. I reckon it's a dirty way to kill.'

'Any way of killing's dirty, mister,' Cody replied gently.

'I agree with you,' said the black dressed man. 'Does not the good book say, "Thou shalt not kill".'

'That's sometimes kind of hard to avoid, mister,' Cody answered. 'When a man's coming at you, dead set on killing you. I saw you on the San Ramos reservation, didn't I?'

'I was there. I'm Samuel Hodges and I was engaged on bringing the Word to the heathens.'

Cody Yarrow did not smile, although he held strong views on people who tried to convert the Apache from a perfectly sound and practical religion because it did not conform with the beliefs of the white man. He looked at Bertha Ford and her niece, waiting for them to introduce themselves.

Caroline spoke for she could see her aunt did not mean to. Cody Yarrow might be a pleasant-sounding young man but he was also a member of the Sieber Apache Scouts, a regiment her aunt had stated committed every act of atrocity and outrage human flesh could contrive against its fellows. So Caroline did not mind her aunt not offering her name. Cody Yarrow sounded proud of the fact that he rode in the Apache Scouts and would want no part of Bertha Ford – or her niece. Caroline suddenly felt how lonely the past weeks had been and wanted to talk with the others, especially the friendly young man called Cody Yarrow.

The others waited for Bertha but Caroline said, 'I'm Caroline Banders and this is my aunt.'

She left it at that and felt surprised that the others did not press for further information. She did not know the code of the west. An offer of introduction could be made but need not be answered and, if it was not there could be no further seeking of information. To the other passengers Bertha clearly did not wish for any part of their company and they accepted her decision.

'Which only leaves the sleeping beauty here,' Julie remarked, turning to Waco, noting the hat drawn over his face as she nudged him gently in the ribs. 'At least I think he's a sleeping beauty, can't tell with that Stetson over his face. Hey, mister, we're getting to know each other.'

Waco stirred, shoved back his hat slightly, looking around with sleep-blurred eyes, grunted, 'Howdy!' drew back the hat brim and settled down again.

Julie turned to the other passengers with a smile. 'Well, that's the first time I ever had one go to sleep on me.'

'I'll wake him if you like,' Wilson put in, ever willing to impress a young woman he planned to know better and exploit to his own profit.

'Leave him be, you don't have to impress anybody with how tough you are,' Julie replied.

Wilson scowled at the young woman and sat angrily back in his seat. Julie relaxed and her smile died for a moment. She had been at San Ramos fort while Wilson gambled with the soldiers, and had his measure. Julie knew Wilson's type, had seen it in a dozen and more towns. He left her strictly alone for he knew she would never fall for his kind. Julie was an entertainer, a fair singer but nothing more. It took a soldier's busted head, via a bottle wielded by Julie's hand, to persuade the men at the fort that song and dance was all the entertainment she gave. She had sense enough to steer clear of Wilson's kind. It came as something of a surprise to find he had left the fort in a hurry but Julie did not attribute the departure to her leaving. Julie had her suspicions about the reasons for Wilson's departure but she kept them to herself.

The coach had now left Albion City behind and lurched at a fair speed over the wheel-rutted trail to the east. Driver and guard both knew this route and expected an easy run.

The passengers settled down in what comfort they could manage. Julie leaned back and closed her eyes, thinking of the next town. She was a sensible young woman and knew that although her act was well received in the small towns she did not have the quality which made a star. Soon, very soon, she would need to get out of the entertaining game and settle down, or drag the rest of her years around the circuit getting older and sinking lower.

A smile came to Julie's lips as she opened her eyes and saw the ground cut from under Wilson's feet by Caroline asking a question about the passing range. The gambler knew little or nothing about the open country, his time being spent inside saloons, watching the fall of pasteboards on the green baize cloth of a card table. Cody Yarrow on the other hand was in his element. This was a land he knew and he pointed out things of interest to Caroline and bringing a flush of pleasure to her cheeks.

Bertha sat back with tight drawn lips and unfriendly eyes. There was none to whom she might speak, not even the gaunt preacher. She sat in silence as did the preacher. Sweat ran freely down his face as he nursed the thick bible and stared into space.

Through it all Waco stayed fast asleep for Julie sat still so as not to disturb him. She had seen his eyes when he shoved his hat back and knew what made them so dull. In saloons Julie often saw drunks and knew the difference between a man sleeping off a load of coffin-varnish and one dog-tired from long, sustained effort. The young cowhand had not been drinking. He bore the look of a man who badly needed sleep so she let him get it.

Waco must have been asleep for all of five hours when he awoke. He stayed in the same position, in a lazy half-sleeping, half-waking way which allowed him to hear and be aware of everything going on around without the burden of joining in the conversation.

The trail passed through rolling, hilly country now, big rocks, dips and ridges causing the coach to wind around. The driver brought his team around a corner, well clear of a large bush so he could see the trail ahead. He gave a startled curse, hauled on the reins and booted home the brake all in one fast-done move. The guard came awake and alert – a full ten seconds too late.

The hold-up had been neatly planned and laid out. Two masked men stood in the centre of the trail, Winchesters lining

25

on the driver and guard. A third man was to one side of the trail, holding a Colt and in a position where he could cover the passengers.

The coach came to a halt in the open around the corner. There was some room on either side of the trail, then the bushes closed in once more. The guard sat still, hands lifting from his shotgun. Under the barrels of two rifles and with a coach full of passengers, he could take no chances.

Leaping forward the pistol-armed outlaw jerked open the coach door and threw down on the passengers.

'Sit fast, all of you!' he ordered in a voice brittle with excitement.

'Do it,' Cody Yarrow, nearest to the door, warned gently. He could see the gambler's face flush with anger and knew any attempt to move might start the young outlaw throwing lead without regard for where it went or who caught it.

The two men with the rifles closed in slightly. Like their companion they wore cowhand dress although they looked older. Both gave the impression they could call their shots at that range so the guard stayed still.

'All right,' said the taller outlaw. 'Toss down your guns.'

The guard licked his lips nervously but complied. He knew the danger of tossing a shotgun from the coach to the ground. On landing the jar might cause a barrel to discharge which in turn would scare the team and could start them running. Or the explosion might trigger off the nerves of the outlaws, who did not look like that would need much doing, and start them throwing lead. So he tossed the shotgun into the bushes at the side of the open land, letting out a breath of relief when it landed and slid to the ground without firing. His revolver followed the shotgun, then the driver's worn old Army Colt.

'Get them out, Joey,' ordered the taller outlaw.

'All right,' said the youngster. 'Pile out all of you and keep your hands held high.'

Cody Yarrow came out first, hands clasped on his hat. He moved away from the coach and towards where the shotgun lay. The young outlaw stepped back as Cody rose, presenting no chance to jump him. Neither he nor the other two gave the impression of being top-grade stock in their line but they were good enough to be deadly dangerous and just scared enough to panic if everything did not go smoothly.

One glance at the shotgun and revolvers told Cody Yarrow the guard and driver could be counted out. That left the gambler and himself for Cody did not count the preacher in and the sleeping man's reactions might be too slow when he woke to be of any help.

'Get them out faster, Joey,' ordered the taller man.

Growling an order for more speed the young outlaw moved nearer to the door. The women climbed down and went towards the men who now stood in line. Joey let them by and looked inside the coach.

'There's another in here, Pat,' he called, 'Sleeping!'

'Well get him out. Watch how you wake him.'

Cody Yarrow and the other passengers halted in a rough line, the men with their hands clasped on their hat tops and the women huddled together, standing with their backs to the bushes. Cody threw a glance at the shotgun which rested on the branches of a bush close at hand. All he needed was a brief diversion and he could reach the gun in one leaping dive. Then he could make things real interesting for the outlaws.

Leaning into the coach Joey gave a wild yell. He saw the tall young Texan start as if the noise woke him, Joey hoped for some reaction which might justify his shooting the man down. That would really be something, to be able to cut his first butt-notch and claim he had stopped the cowhand's attempt to bust up their try at robbing the stage.

Waco gave him no such chance. He was fully awake before the yell and studied the young outlaw from under his hat-brim, reading Joey for what he was. It took more than a drawn-up bandana to prevent him from recognizing a trigger-wild kid just itching for an excuse to throw lead. So Waco moved slowly and carefully, giving a better than fair impersonation of a man just awakened from deep sleep. Stirring in his seat Waco thrust back his hat, rubbing his eyes with both hands in plain sight all the time. He peered sleepily at the open door, blinking and muttering:

'Huh—what—where—'

'On your feet and keep your hands high, cow-nurse,' growled Joe, hefting the Colt to emphasize his words. 'Out of the door.'

Waco rose slowly, keeping his hands clear of his guns as he made for the door in a fumble-footed and half-asleep way. He wanted to make the young outlaw impatient enough to act without thinking. Once that happened he would make a mistake and give Waco a chance. Joey drew back a couple of paces, muttering restlessly.

Still moving slowly Waco came to the door and stood rubbing his eyes as if sleep still held him incapable of fast movement. He jumped down and stumbled. The young outlaw stepped forward, thrusting his Colt into Waco's back with the intention of livening him up.

He got his wish!

Waco leaned back slightly on the muzzle of the Colt, then pivoted fast. He felt the barrel of the gun moving and his left hand lashed down, behind him, slamming into steel and deflecting the Colt away. Joey's startled yell was drowned by the roar of the Colt and Waco felt the muzzle-blast but knew he was not hit for he started to dive aside even as he struck the gun. The taller outlaw brought up his rifle and fired, flame lancing towards the coach. In mid-air Waco heard a yell of pain and surprise from the young outlaw. He did not have time to worry about this for his right hand brought out the right side Colt even as he fell to the ground. The Colt crashed, bucking in his hand, a bullet leaving its five and a half long barrel. The taller outlaw spun around, his rifle falling from his hands even as he tried to lever another bullet into the chamber.

On the ground Waco carried on rolling, left hand also bringing out a Colt for he knew he lived on borrowed time. He thumb-cocked the second Colt, twisting to line it on where, by his reckoning, Joey should be holding a gun ready to throw lead at him. By all fair averages the young outlaw should be on balance now and cutting in, Waco thought and could not decide why he was not.

Landing flat on his back Waco saw why he was still alive. Joey, down on his knees, held his ribs and whimpered in pain, his revolver laying on the ground by his side. It took Waco only a second to know what had happened. The rifleman's fast-taken shot went where aimed, only Waco had left that spot an instant before. The bullet missed and caught Joey a nasty nick across the side. Ironically Waco owed his life to the man he killed for without his bullet Joey would have been able to cut down the young Ranger.

At the moment Waco made his move Cody Yarrow took the chance it offered. The two outlaws gave Waco their full attention and even as one went down Cody hurled himself to a side. He caught up the shotgun and slewed around swinging the gun up, the double barrels slapping into his left palm. The remaining outlaw hesitated, not knowing for sure which menace to deal with first. The pause cost him his life. He started to bring around the rifle to down Cody but never had a chance. The shotgun boomed while held waist high and the nine-buckshot charge lashed across the man's body throwing him into the bushes, his rifle triggering off a shot which went into the air.

The scene felt strangely silent after the roar of shots. Waco started to come to his feet, sparing a glance at the women. Caroline stood with her face buried in Julie's hair while the rusty-haired woman held and comforted her like a child. Bertha Ford stood rigid, her eyes dilated with horror as she stared around from one to another of the participants in the deadly corpse-and-cartridge affair. The Reverend Hodges stood slightly away from the rest, still holding the bible in both hands. Frank Wilson stood still too, he had not made a move to draw his gun as yet.

With an animal snort Wilson lunged forward, the short barrelled Mervin & Hulbert gun sliding into his hand. The gambler moved towards Joey, his thumb drawing back the hammer of the revolver.

'You lousy scum!' he hissed, aiming at the young outlaw's head. 'I'll kill you for—'

Waco had been about to move in and disarm Joey but Wilson was ahead of him. The young Texan snapped out: 'Hold it!'

'Keep out of this, cow-nurse,' Wilson snarled back. 'No lousy owlhoot's going to throw down on me and live to boast about it.'

'Leather it, hombre,' Waco ordered, seeing the bloodlust on Wilson's face and in his eyes. 'Or turn it this way.'

Wilson turned slightly, facing Waco at the words. The young Texan stood on his feet and full ready to meet whatever play Wilson made. The way he stood told Wilson that. Feet slightly apart, knees bent and body crouched to offer a smaller target. The centre of the young Texan, lined full on Wilson's body, was the bore of his right hand Colt. In that instant Wilson knew he did not deal with a cowhand trying to impress anybody. Here stood a lawman.

'No lousy owlhoot's going to rob me,' Wilson repeated, not lowering his gun and not seeing the glint in Joey's eyes.

'It's your choice,' replied Waco. 'Call it whichever way you want.'

For all his words Waco knew the danger he faced. The young outlaw might still be on his knees but he no longer made a sound. In a moment, unless disarmed, he would make a grab at the gun and try to kill his way out of the spot he found himself in.

Wilson hesitated, although the temptation to kill stayed with him, kicking at his nerves, begging him to make a move. Yet for all that he held his hand knowing the only way he could kill the outlaw would be to drop the young Texan first.

'You might get one of us, gambling man,' Cody Yarrow cut in, swinging his shotgun and cocking back the unfired barrel's hammer. 'But it'll be hell trying to decide which one first.'

At that moment Joey saw his chance and took it. He knew all attention had been diverted from him and he would never have a better chance. His hand drove down, closed on the butt of the gun and he dived to one side, fanning the hammer as he went. He did not know where the shots were going and cared less. He was scared, and like a rat in a trap attacked blindly, striking without worrying over whom he struck.

Three times the gun roared, the bullets lashing the air around Waco and narrowly missing the women. Then Waco turned and fired through the powdersmoke which wrapped and wafted around Joey. The young outlaw reared up, the force of the .45 bullet almost lifting him to his feet – but he still held his gun. Waco acted like the trained lawman he was. Joey still held his gun, kept his feet and was as dangerous as ever. The bandana had slipped, showing his features, not much more than seventeen years old, or his face lied. Old or young he could still squeeze a trigger or slap back the hammer. So Waco fired again, throwing his lead into Joey's head and sending him down.

'No!' Bertha Ford screamed. 'NO!'

The outlaw's body pitched over even as the words left her lips. She moved forward, by Waco who stood with smoke dribbling up from the barrel of his Colt, and looked down at Joey. The outlaw lay spread-eagled on the ground his face young looking and innocent now death clouded and removed the killer glare in his eyes. For a moment Bertha Ford looked down at the outlaw then turned to Waco.

'Murderer!' she hissed.

If Waco heard he gave no sign. He holstered his matched guns and turned to face Wilson as the gambler slid his Merwin & Hulbert back under his arm.

'You stupid, no-good skunk!' Waco said, his voice throbbing with anger.

'What's wrong with you?' Wilson replied harshly. 'He's not the first you've had to cut down.'

Waco moved in. His right fist drove out to crash into the gambler's face and sent him sprawling to the ground. Wilson lit down hard on his back, his hand went under his arm. Cody Yarrow stepped forward, bringing down the shotgun to press on the gambler's arm, holding the gun in its shoulder clip.

'Don't make him kill you!' Yarrow snapped.

Working his fingers to get the stiffness out of them Waco moved forward to stand over Wilson.

'That kid died through you and for no good reason,' he gritted. 'You gave him time to get his nerve back. I could've taken him alive if you hadn't.'

'So what?' Wilson spat out, getting to his feet. 'He was on the prod, just looking for a chance to kill. You saw that yourself.'

Yarrow caught Waco by the arm and held him. 'We've got to move the coach, *amigo*,' he said gently. 'This is no place for the women.'

Slowly the anger left Waco. He looked to where Julie led Caroline to the coach. The driver and guard had climbed down and they helped Caroline inside for the girl was close to hysteria. Bertha Ford followed, throwing a look as she entered the coach at the tall young Texan who had saved their lives. Wilson turned and was about to go to the coach when Waco snapped:

'Not you, *hombre*. These three have to be buried and you're helping with it.'

For a moment it seemed Wilson would object. Then he saw the determined look on Waco's face and the cold gleam in Cody Yarrow's eyes. He knew they stood together and would make him wish he had obeyed without argument if he gave them trouble. The driver brought a pick and shovel from the coach's boot and with a contemptuous gesture tossed the shovel to Wilson.

'Dig or walk, it's all one to me.'

Waco turned to the gaunt preacher. 'You'd best come along, Reverend,' he said. 'Say a few words over them.'

'I suppose even the ungodly such as these need that,' replied Hodges.

The bodies were carried into the bushes for burying while in the coach the women sat in silence for a time. Julie looked at Bertha Ford and asked:

'Aren't you going to say anything to your niece?'

'Let her cry it out,' Bertha replied, lips tight and grim. 'I'll say what I have to say in private.'

'She could use some comfort now,' Julie stated. 'Easy now, honey. It's all over and done with.'

Bertha looked at Julie and her lips tightened again but she did not offer to speak either to her or to Caroline. Time passed and the men returned, the passengers climbing into the coach while the guard fastened three saddled horses to the rear. Then he took up his shotgun, checked the boot fastenings and climbed on top.

The coach lurched on its way again and for a time none of the passengers spoke. Suddenly Bertha Ford jerked erect in her seat, her forefinger pointing at Waco.

'You! I recognize you now. You're the one I saw this morning, coming into Albion. Driving three men before you just like they were animals.'

'Yes, ma'am,' agreed Waco, seeing a clash and not side-stepping it. 'Just like that.'

'This here's Waco, ma'am,' Cody Yarrow put in. 'He's an Arizona Ranger.'

The words were ill-timed and did nothing to help the situation. The Arizona Rangers owed their existence to the Democrat Governor of the Territory and in Bertha Ford's eyes that meant they were a political force, a private police with powers exceeding those of county sheriffs and even United States marshals.

'You drove those prisoners like cattle,' she went on savagely. 'Then you killed that child back there. Shot him down without a chance.'

'Now hold hard there, ma'am,' growled Cody Yarrow. 'Waco shot because he had to shoot. He cut that boy down, sure, but it was the boy or his own life.'

'Self-defence,' sneered Mrs. Ford. 'The cry of the protected killer behind a law badge. Was he driving those three men for self-defence too?'

'Yes, ma'am, I was,' Waco replied. 'Those three and two more raided a small town bank. They lost their heads inside and shot down two fellers and an old woman. Shot them in self-defence, way you're calling it, even though none of them three folks had a gun. Then they killed a deputy, a white haired old timer who held a star like he'd done for so many years he just couldn't do no other work at all. He was one of those protected killers behind a law-badge, likely. I was on hand, took after them and they ran. They killed four hosses running from me and lost the fifth when I caught up with them. Those three I brought in were all that I could. They allowed to jump me as soon as I stopped to sleep and I allowed they wouldn't. So we didn't stop. Yeah, I reckon I drove them like cattle for self-defence.'

'You killed two men of the gang and two back there,' Bertha

Fort gasped. 'Four men in less than a week. What gives you that right. By what authority do you set up as judge, jury and executioner?'

'I'm an Arizona Ranger, ma'am. I do things the way I have to.'

'The way *you* see fit to, you mean. Four men lay dead because *you* saw fit.'

'Yes, ma'am, and I'm still alive. Way I see it my life's valuable and any man who tries to kill me's got to be stopped, even if I have to kill him. Why? No reason except that I'm important to me. I could have stood by and let those three back there rob us. Likely they'd done it and gone without giving us trouble. But what about the next job they pulled, or the one after that? Some day they'd hit on a man who tried to fight back. They'd spook and throw lead wild, maybe kill some innocent gal, or old man who happened to be near by when the shooting started. Way I saw it I was paid to take the chance. As long as I could do it without getting you folks hurt I'd got to stop those three afore they killed me – or somebody else.'

'So you, with your God-given right, killed them,' she hissed. 'One of them was a boy of not more than seventeen.'

'He'd got a gun, ma'am and knew how to use it. That made him a man-growed. At seventeen I held a law badge in Mulrooney and did a man's work. In New Mexico right now, ma'am, there's a boy of seventeen who's killed at least eight men. His name's Bill Bonney, you likely heard of him as Billy the Kid.'

'What of it?'

'You can't tell me about killers no matter what age, ma'am,' Waco replied. 'I've lived most all my growing years among men who've used guns and killed. That boy back there stood full growed with a gun in his hand. He wanted to shoot his way clear, to kill, and he wasn't bothered which of us he killed. Me, you, the preacher, any of us, didn't make no never mind as long as he killed. That kind has to be stopped fast, ma'am. He died there this afternoon but likely other folks'll live the safer for it.'

'Words!' the woman hissed back, not another of the passengers speaking as they watched Waco face her. 'The same excuses I've heard from professional killers with badges given by Democrat power-seekers—'

'Stop it!' Caroline screamed out the words, coming to her feet and facing her aunt. 'Aunt Bertha, you've said and done enough. Must your hatred for the Democrats be brought into

33

everything and against everybody you meet! You've ruined my life for years. Don't try and ruin it any more.'

Bertha turned amazed eyes to her niece. 'Caroline,' she gasped. 'How do you mean, ruined your life?'

'You have!' the girl replied. 'What life have I ever had. Never allowed to mix with people of my own kind because their parents were Democrats. What kind of friends did I have? The college students you and your kind paid to educate. What sort of friends were they? Intelligent and nothing more, hating everyone who had anything they did not, despising the working class people they came from. They were the worst snobs in the world, with nothing but intelligence that had no purpose except to ruin anyone better placed. They were the friends I had. That was why I came West with you. I wanted to meet people, decent, friendly people, not boorish intellectuals. So I came West with you and I wish to God I had not.'

For the first time in her life Bertha Ford felt uncomfortable as she tried and failed to meet her niece's hate-filled eyes. 'I—don't understand you.'

'You don't know, do you!' Caroline answered. 'You're so blindly egotistical you can't see beyond your own nose. Look at me, Aunt Bertha. Look at me. I'm a good looking woman, I'm young, I'm still not too old to be happy. Yet at the only dance we attended, at Fort Becket, the partners I had were ordered to dance with me by the commanding officer. I heard the other women laughing about it. They danced but they would not speak to me and you know why. Because I'm Bertha Ford's niece and anything they said might be twisted into lies and sent East to be published in some mud-slinging newspaper. It was the same everywhere I went. Nobody wanted to speak with Bertha Ford's niece. I've not had a pleasant word spoken to me until we boarded this stage and now you've spoiled that. These people know who I am. They know if they talk to me they might say the wrong thing. They know you're waiting, like you waited with that half-breed interpreter for every un-supported Apache story, without checking the facts as long as they were derogatory to the Army. And why, because the Army serves the Democrats in your eyes. Not because they're taking some lives, or because you really care what happens to the Apaches. I'm sick of lies and I'm more than sick of you!'

With that the girl turned, tears trickling down her cheeks. She felt two arms around her and heard Julie whispering to her to sit down. The full flood of her emotion burst like a flood. She sank to the seat by Julie and sobbed in the other woman's arms.

34

Bertha Ford met the eyes of the men with what defiance she could manage. The gambler and the gaunt preacher displayed little interest but the other two showed their cold dislike for both had been part of a force which felt the lash of her printed words. They knew who she was now and wondered what drove her to hunt out any kind of story as long as they were discreditable to the law officers or army.

'Well,' she hissed. 'Now you know who I am. Do you wish you'd let that boy kill me?'

'No, ma'am,' Waco replied. 'I'd've stopped him even knowing who you are. It would've been my job. Why'd you hate us, ma'am? We've work to do, dirty work and we play it the only way we can. Sure, there's some who'd play dirty come what may, I'm not denying it. I've known lawmen who'd cut down a man without asking two words, if they thought he needed taking in. Hickok was one and he was no Democrat. His sort don't last long. Sooner or later the decent folk of that sort's town want real law and they move him on. It happened to Hickok in Hays and Abilene. It'll happen to the Earps in Tombstone in the end.'

'You work as a hired killer for the Democrat—'

'No, ma'am. Least ways, as far as I know, never having gotten round to asking him, Cap'n Mosehan's a Republican. Me, I'm maybe a year too young to vote but I'll like vote Democrat when I do. That won't stop me respecting Cap'n Bert, taking his orders and doing whatever I have to do no matter what party's in at the territorial capital.'

'What makes you hate Democrats, ma'am?' Cody Yarrow asked. 'I've seen some politicians from both sides, they allus seemed to get on friendly enough away from the voting floor.'

'Why do I hate them?' Bertha replied, her voice low and throbbing. 'They killed my husband. A drunken mob of Democrats took my husband out and hung him from a tree. And you ask why I hate Democrats.'

With that she sank into her seat, face set and rigid without a touch of colour to it. The other passengers did not speak to each other and apart from the ever present sound of hooves, the creak of leather and the groans of the timber of the coach, only Caroline's sobs joined the clicking as Waco turned the cylinder of his Colt, ejecting the empty cases and replacing them with live bullets for his task had not ended yet.

Outside the sun sank slowly and in the distance the lights of Randle's Way Station glowed invitingly.

35

Randle's Way Station lay by the side of a fair sized river, just where it formed a lake. The area looked like a green oasis after the harsh and arid land the coach traversed during the day. The Way Station, a long, cool looking and sizeable building was a haven of rest for travellers. To one side lay an adobe walled corral where the spare teams and horses of visitors were kept. To the other side rose the *jacales* of some dozen or so workers of mixed Mexican-Apache blood. For some strange reason no lights showed from the *jacales*, they stayed silent and deserted as the coach came to a halt before the Station building.

Ma Randle stepped from the open door of the building, a double-barrelled ten gauge in her hands. She looked towards the coach in a cautious manner which did not leave until she recognized the driver.

'Howdy, Shotgun, Mick,' she greeted.

The driver looked around. There should have been a purposeful bustle about the place, peons running up to unhitch the team and help unload such luggage as the passengers needed for the night. Only there were no peons, nothing but Ma Randle with her shotgun and her wolf-cautious stare.

'Where's Pedro and the boys, Ma?' asked the driver who went by the name of Shotgun. 'Or do we have to unhitch our own team now?'

'That's just what you have to do,' she replied.

Ma Randle stood six feet, a mountain of a woman with the heft and muscles of a hard-rock miner. Her hair was grey, her face tanned oak brown but still retaining something of a large beauty. The big body might bulk and strain inside the gingham dress but Ma had little surplus fat, it was hard firm flesh and the arms rolled with such muscles as a strong man might not be ashamed to possess.

She ran the Way Station, aided by her tiny husband although Ma did all the heavy toting around the place. From the look of her and her general attitude the words had much truth in them. One thing nobody could say about Ma was that she did not know her work. The fact that no peons were on hand to help unhitch the team did not mean Ma was unaware they should be. She kept the Station going and usually the peons hopped to obey her orders like fleas on a griddle.

'What's wrong, Ma?' asked the driver, knowing her of old. 'You got some trouble here?'

'Not yet. Get your folks out and into the house, then put those hosses in the corral. There's plenty of room.'

Waco did not stand on ceremony and left the coach ahead of the women, with Cody Yarrow hard on his heels. Ma Randle looked them over and a flickering expression came to her face as she recognized them.

'Howdy Ranger, Cody,' she greeted. 'You're as welcome as water in the desert. How many more inside?'

'Five, Ma,' Waco replied. 'Something wrong?'

'Nothing much. 'Cepting that every head of hosses went last night and come dawn Pedro pulled out with the peons. Then when I thought to wire for the company to send a trouble-shooter along, I couldn't get through, the wires were down. I sent Pa out to find the break in the line and he found it all right. Over a hundred foot of it cut and gone.'

'Which starts to sound like Apaches,' Waco drawled, then stopped speaking as the other passengers climbed from the coach. There was no sense in starting a panic for the station was in no immediate danger.

'Inside, folks, food's waiting,' Ma boomed, ushering the women into the building.

Wilson and the preacher followed the women inside, leaving Waco and Yarrow on the porch watching the cursing stage crew unhitch the team. Ma turned to go after her guests, then halted and looked at the three saddle-horses. None of them belonged to Waco or Yarrow. Neither the Rangers nor Apache Scouts would use such sorry specimens; and no self-respecting Texan rode a single-girth, ventre-fire saddle, claiming such were fit only for green dudes and other Yankees.

'You run into trouble?' she asked.

'Some,' Waco replied. 'I'll tell you about it later. Reckon it was Apaches who took off with your stock?'

'I was down there and checked. Just about enough sign for it to be Apache work.'

It never occurred to either man to doubt Ma's judgment of the situation. She had been over thirty years in Arizona Territory and never lived anyplace that a woman did not need to be able to handle a rifle as well as a skillet. Ma knew how to read sign as well as many a man while her Apache-knowledge could exceed that of a number of well-known Indian-fighting army officers.

'I don't get it, Ma,' Yarrow put in. 'The San Ramos's the nearest Apache reservation. I was through there a couple of days back and nary a sign of raiding showed.'

'That's what I'd've thought until this morning,' Ma Randle answered. 'But I got certain sure it was Apaches when I found the *jacales* empty and Pedro's kin all lit out.'

That figured. The peons had inter-married with Apaches for generations and had an insight into the tribe's behaviour. They would catch signs, or might even have received a friendly word of warning to pull up stakes and get out. In either case they would leave fast.

'We can't get to do anything afore dawn, Ma,' Waco drawled. 'Today's team'll get us to Mecate and we can wire the cavalry. You coming with us?'

'It'd take a sight more than a few Apaches to chase us out of here,' Ma answered grimly. 'Now take it easy in there and don't scare the folks. I don't want no hysterical women on my hands.'

The main room of the Way Station contained bar, saloon and dining-room. At the back lay the bedrooms for the male and female passengers, the Randles' quarters and kitchen. The bar end of the room was separated from the rest of the building by a chalk line. Beyond the line a travelling lady could sit without the taint of entering a saloon. The line did not look much of a barrier but, under Ma's strong rule, stood as sturdy as a wall built of solid rock.

Bertha Ford sat alone, her niece having neither spoken to her nor acknowledged her presence since sinking to her seat in the coach. Caroline shared a table with Julie, her eyes still red but her face regaining its smile as she got control of herself once more. Hodges also sat alone, his bible unopened on the table. Wilson stood at the bar, sullenly eyeing Waco and waiting to be served.

'What's wrong, Waco?' asked Julie as he and Cody Yarrow approached her table.

'Nothing at all, Miss Julie,' lied Waco.

Yet things were wrong, bad wrong. It was not just a chance raid which left the Way Station without spare horses. The Apaches wanted the coach holding and Waco knew why.

'But you seem so concerned about something, Mr. Waco,' Caroline put in.

Waco grinned, looking about fifteen years old. 'Know something, Miss Bander, ma'am, I've never been called mister afore.'

Caroline's cheek flushed just a little red at the words. She suddenly realized that Julie and the two men did not hold her relationship with Bertha Ford against her. The two men held their hats in their hands, then asked for permission to sit down.

'Feel free,' replied Julie. 'And Caroline, you only call a man mister out here if you don't like him. What *is* wrong, Waco. I've been to Ma Randle's more than once and never seen the stage driver unhitch his own team before.'

'Waal, I'll let you into a secret,' replied Waco, dropping his voice in a confidential manner. 'It's Pa Randle.'

'What'd he do?' asked Julie, eternal woman, hot and eager for gossip.

'Took off with Pedro's squaw. Upped and threw her across the back of his hoss and headed for the hills. So ole Pedro and the rest just took out after them.'

'Am I supposed to believe that?' snorted Julie.

'It's as true as I'm riding this here bull buffalo,' Waco replied. 'Cross my heart and hope to vote Republican.'

There was just a momentary embarrassed pause for Waco realized Caroline's loyalties might be to the Republican party and Texas-style jokes about were not in the best of taste. Caroline only laughed and put him at ease in the manner of a born diplomat. The truth of Waco's statement went bouncing to the floor when Pa Randle entered, a large tray loaded with steaming plates across one arm. Caroline studied the small, weedy, inoffensive looking man and asked how he managed to lift a woman on to the back of a horse.

Chuckling, Julie explained that Pedro's squaw, while smaller, weighed even more than Ma Randle and it would take a good horse to carry her off at a gallop, assuming Pa had the strength and desire to swoop her up and head for the hills.

'It's cowhand humour, Caroline,' Julie finished. 'They're like overgrown schoolkids, all of them.'

The plates were set before Caroline and Julie first, Pa serving with speed that told of long practice. The plates contained a thick and appetizing stew, the steam of which gave off a pleasant aroma and made Caroline's mouth water for she had eaten nothing since breakfast.

'What is this stew?' she asked.

'We call it son-of-a-b—gun stew,' Cody replied, hastily changing the range title for something more suited to female ears. He heard Julie's gurgle of held down amusement for she knew the correct name. 'See, the cook takes just about any old thing he can lay hand on, throws them in the pot with the choice cuts of a calf, then cooks the lot until you can't tell what any son-of-a-gun of it is. Then he serves it up red hot or all hands want to know why not.'

The stew tasted as good as it looked and smelled. Caroline could never remember when she enjoyed a meal so much for the conversation held her attention and brought tears of laughter to her face. She had never been really close to the people of the West before and found that three at least were not uncouth savages whose only aim in life was to shed the blood of fellow human beings. Then she remembered that both men had shed blood that same afternoon, taken life before her very eyes. Yet they spoke of the humorous part of their lives, showing her a side to them she never suspected a man who killed could have. In a few minutes Caroline learned more about human nature than in all her previous life.

Julie pushed her plate away and sat back, laughter sparkling in her eyes. 'Come on, Caroline,' she said. 'Let's freshen up, then we can come back and listen to these pair spinning some more windies.'

Collecting their overnight bags from the porch the two women went into the sideroom reserved for female passengers. Inside were four beds, each with clean sheets and blankets. In one corner stood a wash basin and Ma Randle entered with a large jug of hot water.

'Here you are, gals,' she said, putting it by the washstand. 'Make yourselves at home.'

Caroline washed and tidied up first and while waiting for Julie to finish took the thick letter from her bag. She looked down at the sealed back flap for a long moment then shrugged and thrust the letter unopened into the bag once more. Somehow the information inside did not seem to be important any more. Julie had completed her freshening up and they returned to the main room. Cody Yarrow left the group at the bar, crossed the room and joined them. Bertha Ford sat alone, her brooding eyes on her niece. She knew that Caroline had left her now and would be unlikely to return unless she made the first move but her pride would not allow her to make it.

'Tell you, Waco,' said Shotgun, nursing his glass of beer, the only drink Ma allowed a driver with a run to make, 'Was it any other place but this I'd be real worried.'

'I'm worried now,' Waco replied. 'What do you make of it, Mick?'

'Took all into consideration,' replied the guard sagely. 'I'd say we was in for a tolerable slew of Apache trouble.'

'Sure,' agreed Waco. 'And you could be right at that. I'll just take a walk to the corral and have a look at the horses.'

'Want company?' asked the guard.

'About two regiments of Confederate cavalry'd be fine. Can't have them so I reckon I'll go alone. I'm not all that scared of the dark.'

Waco turned and walked from the room. Wilson stood at the far end of the bar, nursing a bottle and glowering at the others. He let his hand slide under his coat towards the butt of the revolver but did not draw it. Wilson might be drunk but he could still think. The moment he drew and shot at the Ranger he would be dead, for the others would not stand by and allow murder to go unpunished.

Outside the night was dark and still, not even the stars giving any light as Waco came from the building and looked towards the unhitched coach. He stepped forward, passing the coach and making for the corral. Every instinct warned him that something was wrong. The corral loomed ahead, bulking black against the dark of the night. It lay silent – too silent.

Like most buildings in this tree-stunted land, the corral was constructed of adobe mud, stood six foot high and sturdy enough to hold in horses, particularly the heavy horses which drew Wells Fargo coaches and did little jumping. The corral walls would keep the stock in – as long as the gate remained closed.

Waco saw the gate standing open and went forward fast, his hands dropping to his matched guns. The corral held no horses, the six from the coach's team and the three belonging to the dead outlaws were no longer confined within the walls. The driver and guard knew how to handle horses, they would not forget to secure the gate on leaving the animals inside. Waco cursed himself for not posting a guard, then knew that most likely the man would be dead now, had one been on watch.

'Don't turn, white brother!'

The words came from the darkness, floating in the air from nothing it seemed, but Waco knew a very material something was speaking to him. He could sense them all around him. Picture them too, cold-eyed, squat-built, with lank and long black hair, watching him in the darkness, their weapons held ready for use. Only that voice should not be with a bunch of bad-hat Apache horse-thieves. It was the voice of an old friend, of Johnny No-Legs, Apache army scout. For all that it was a warning voice and one which must be obeyed.

'I didn't know you went in for hoss stealing, Johnny,' he said.

'There will be death soon, Ranger. Much death,' came the reply, neither confirming nor denying Waco's words but ignoring them as if they had never been said. 'I have told these who ride with me of how you saved my life and how you caught the man who shot Victorio. That was all which saved you, *amigo*. These others would have taken you and sent you into the house as warning to the white-eyes inside.'

41

'I wouldn't have liked that at all,' Waco replied.

For all the light way in which he spoke Waco felt the hair rise stiff and bristly on the back of his neck. He knew the Apache way of taking a prisoner, putting him to torture, then sending him to their enemies as a warning of what they could expect.

'What're you wanting, Johnny?'

'Mangus Colorado's medicine. One of the white-eyes who came on the stage with you has it.'

'Which one?'

'That I do not know. Nor what the medicine is like. I heard of the stealing and rode fast to try and stop the men of the San Ramos putting on their paint and riding to war. I have talked long and well for they hold until the sun rises. You have until then to find the medicine and return it, with the one who took it.'

Waco stood for a moment without speaking, hoping Johnny could tell him something, anything, that might help find the medicine. For all he heard Waco might have been alone but he knew they still watched him.

'Don't any of the brave-hearts with you know who has the medicine?' he asked.

'None of these here. They are young warriors and ride fast. Only the elders of the tribe know of the medicine. One comes but there is age in his bones and he rides slowly. Perhaps he will come before the sun rises – maybe not.'

'Will you bring him to me when he comes?'

'There is much between us, Ranger?' Johnny No-Legs replied. 'I will do what I can for you. If you hear the call of an owl followed by the bark of a coyote come and I will tell you all I know. But by sun rise, whether the old one comes or not, I can hold in the brave-hearts no longer. If they strike many white-eyes will die. I have saved you, led these with me to hold their hands. I do no more, *amigo*.'

The silence dropped once more like a curtain. For ten minutes Waco stood like a statue, waiting and listening. Once he thought he heard the gentle padding of feet but could not be sure. He remained as he was, still as the gate post against which he stood. At last he allowed his breath to come out in a long sigh of relief. Turning he walked with purposeful strides towards the Way Station.

The time for polite diplomacy, for sitting back and keeping eyes open for some sign, was passed. It went by the moment Johnny No-Legs spoke his words of warning. Out there, invisible in the night, the Apaches waited and watched. It only wanted one bad-hat white-hater among them to blow the entire situation, together with Johnny's promise of holding off until dawn, into the air, and the people in the Way Station would blow up with it.

'You should see Texas at this time of the year, Caroline,' Cody Yarrow told the laughing-eyed girl who sat at his table.

'I saw it two years ago,' she pointed out, then wished she'd not spoken for on that occasion her aunt reported stories of the army's treatment of Kiowa Indians and a full colonel was broken and ruined as a result of it.

'Sure, you saw some of it. Ysaleta County now, there's a land for you.'

Julie sat on the other side of the table, a smile playing on her lips as she watched Caroline and the tanned young scout. Julie believed in romance, even in love, for other people. Then her eyes went to Bertha Ford who still sat alone, resisting any of the few attempts made by the others to draw her into conversation. At another table, also alone and aloof sat the preacher. Julie wondered why he did not offer his help to the woman for she looked as if she needed help from somebody.

'It's not a bad country,' Julie replied. 'I was in Ysaleta one time, singing. The town's fine, growing, the sort of place a woman could settle down in.'

'You settle down, Julie,' laughed Cody. 'That's about as likely as rain in the Staked Plains.'

'Would you like to settle down, Julie?' Caroline asked, wondering what made a pleasant young woman roam the West.

'Sure, one day. What I'd like would be small shop, selling dresses and hats. I've some money saved but not enough to set out on my own.'

Caroline studied Julie for a long time. It had always been her own ambition to own a business house of the kind she'd seen in New York and other big cities. She had learned something of dress designing under a tutor and wondered if she might put it to good use. One thing Caroline knew, she could not return with her aunt but there did not seem any way she could avoid it until Julie spoke. Caroline was trying to put her thoughts into words when the door opened and Waco entered.

Crossing to the bar Waco called Ma along to him. The woman's grin died as she caught the tension on his face.

'I'd like all these folks listening to me, Ma, and some backing from you.'

43

'You've got both,' she replied, coming around the bar to join him. Her method of granting the first request was simple. Throwing back her head she let out a bellow which might have been heard in Albion City had the wind been right, 'Hey, all of you, the Ranger wants to talk to you.'

The room fell silent and all eyes went to the tall young Texan as he stood before them, hands thumb-hooked into his gun-belt.

'Some of you might've been wondering what I'm doing riding a stage. Could've thought it to do with that hold-up. It wasn't, I've been playing my cards close to the vest hoping I'd learn what I wanted without doing what I aim to do right now. One of you passengers took Mangus Colorado's medicine from the San Ramos reservation, and has still got it with him – or her.'

'What are you implying?' Bertha Ford demanded, flipping open the notebook which she had taken from her bag while freshening up.

'I'm not implying anything, ma'am,' Waco replied, 'I'm telling you right straight out what happened. One of you has something the Apaches price high. It's something they're willing to take the warpath over, if they don't get it back.'

'What is this medicine, Waco?' Julie asked, 'Is it valuable?'

'I don't know what it is, but likely it'd sell for a better than fair price in the East. I know an old army scout who used to buy rusted up old rifles, drive tacks in the woodwork and sell them to dudes as real, genuine Indian weapons. He got a thousand dollars for one he claimed was took off Sitting Bull when the army caught him. I reckon a real thing like Mangus Colorado's medicine would bring even more. Do you know what the medicine is, Ma?'

'Nope. I've never seen it, Ranger.'

'You, Cody?'

'I've heard tell of it, Waco,' replied the scout. 'So have most folks who know Apaches. But I've never seen it and I don't reckon any other white man has.'

'We'd best find it for all that,' Ma put in.

There was a rumbling mutter of agreement with the words from driver, guard, Julie and Cody Yarrow. All had seen Apache war and all but Julie helped fight off the savage warriors before the army finally brought peace. They all had a fair idea what store the Apaches set on Mangus Colorado's medicine.

'I aim to make a good try,' Waco promised.

44

'You've no proof one of us has the thing, whatever it is,' snorted Bertha.

'Only the words of my boss, which same's all I want, and a couple of small things. The Apaches watched the hotels you folks stayed at and no others in town. They watched the livery barns and were still watching the Wells Fargo office when we pulled out. Could even have followed us although I've seen none of them. That all spells just one small thing. The Apaches know one of you has the medicine.'

'Which one?' Julie asked as the passengers exchanged looks.

'It could be any one of you,' Waco replied. 'All six of you were on the reservation about the time the medicine went.'

'I never went outside the fort,' Julie remarked, 'I'm a city gal who doesn't like being bounced about on the back of a horse. There's an easy way to find out who has it. Search us all.'

'Which same I aim to do right now,' drawled Waco. 'Shotgun, Mick, go bring all the baggage in here and let the folks sort out their own. Ma—'

Wilson moved from the bar, his face flushed with whisky, dark, ugly and with the slit-eyed mean look of a bad drunk. He braced himself, his hand lifting towards the front of his coat and the butt of the Merwin & Hulbert gun.

'Nobody's going to search me or my bags!' he snarled.

The driver and the guard stood still, so did Ma Randle. Pa Randle had just entered from the back, carrying a bottle of whisky, but he stopped in his tracks. All had seen a bad drunk before and knew the danger of crossing such a man. Waco also knew the danger, knew it and took it without backing an inch. His voice was soft, cold and impersonal as he faced the gambler.

'Mister, drunk, sober, dead or alive, I'm searching you.'

The gambler's eyes locked with Waco's. Cold hate boiled up inside Wilson, stoked by the Randle's whisky. The rest of the room was a blank, only the tall Texan having any substance. That man had humiliated him, struck him down, made him look dirt in front of Caroline Banders. Slowly Wilson's fingers worked, forming the shape in which they would close around the butt of his revolver. Then suddenly the whisky went cold in his stomach as he could almost see the way Waco's hands brought out his guns in that whirling blur of action in the afternoon. He could remember the way Waco moved, the speed with which he deflected the young outlaw's gun, flung himself to one side, drawing while falling and throwing his lead accurately even as he landed. Half a second, that was all the time elapsed but in it the Ranger's gun came clear of leather and killed a man.

Suddenly Wilson's lips were very dry and he ran a tongue tip over them. The rest of the room came into focus again. He stood fast for all that, hand still ready to haul out his gun.

Pa Randle moved, seeing the danger and acting on it. 'Hey!' he called and tossed the whisky bottle towards Wilson.

Seeing the bottle coming at him Wilson made an involuntary gesture. His hands came together, catching the bottle then releasing it again. His right hand moved back in the direction of his gun. Waco came in, the Colt which slid into his left hand rose and fell in a fast chopping motion that laid the barrel against Wilson's already swollen jaw. The gambler's knees folded under him and he crashed to the floor.

'Thanks, Pa,' said Waco, bending to pull the Merwin & Hulbert from under Wilson's arm and tuck it into his belt.

'I never could stand a man who can't hold his likker,' replied Pa, with a cackle like a hen laying two eggs at once. He looked at the bottle which Wilson dropped and cackled again. 'That's truer than I meant. I brought the bottle for him and he sure didn't hold it for long.'

Waco did not laugh. 'Get the bags in here, will you,' he said. 'Ma, take the ladies in their room and search them.'

'I thought you'd search us,' sneered Bertha Ford, her hatred showing plain.

'Why for, ma'am. I've seen a woman with no clothes on, it's no novelty. I don't reckon you'd have any more to show, or different from any other woman so I'll let Ma search you. Like the rules say.'

'How dare you!' the woman hissed. 'You come here accusing me—'

'Simmer down,' Ma growled, moving forward and thrusting her large face almost into Bertha Ford's. 'Waco didn't accuse anybody. He's doing something that needs doing and I'm helping him.'

'Do you know who you're speaking to?'

'Who you are and what you are,' Ma replied coolly, 'I don't like either. All your sort are the same, you can insult and abuse who the hell you like. You can break every rule but everybody else has to play them as they suit you. Either of you other ladies object if I search you?'

Julie grinned. 'Not as long as you don't tickle. The sheriff's

46

wife over to Mecate tickles something awful when she searches you.'

'I've no objections,' Caroline went on. 'Nor should you have, Aunt Bertha. You've nothing to hide, have you?'

With that Caroline rose and walked to the baggage, selected her own and followed the driver who carried it into the room at the rear for her. Julie collected her luggage and the guard carried Bertha's bags in. Ma followed the women but paused at the door.

'What am I looking for, Ranger?'

'I'll be Texas-damned if I know, Ma,' Waco admitted. 'Anything that looks Apache. A ring, a bracelet maybe. Could be a medicine pouch or even an old knife or a cap and ball gun. You're as likely to know it as I am if you see it.'

Ma entered the room, closing the door, Pa brought a bucket of water and poured it over the groaning gambler, bringing him into a sitting position, spluttering curses. His hand went to the empty shoulder clip and he came to his feet but moved to the bar and caused no more trouble. The preacher left his table and pointed out his belongings, then stood back to await his turn to be searched.

Cody Yarrow was the first, stripping off all his clothes and handing them to Waco who searched them, then the contents of the scout's warbag. It was the most unusual search Waco had ever made. Often he had checked a suspect's person, and belongings but he had always known what he looked for. This time he searched for something and had no idea for what he searched. He relied on his eyes, on his knowledge of Apaches and a fair bit of luck. The prize for success stood high. As high as the cost of lives and money to put down a full-scale Apache uprising.

In the ladies' room Caroline, blushing a little at having to strip naked before two comparative strangers, sat on the edge of a bed and waited until Ma finished examining her clothes. Then she dressed while Julie, with the casual acceptance of one who regularly changed clothes in a room full of strange women, took off her clothes and passed them to Ma. Then Julie's face reddened and she said:

'There's nothing in my vanity bag, Ma.'

Ma glanced at Julie, surprised at the objection. She opened the bag and took out a ball of wool into which stuck two knitting needles. She spread the needles and looked at the neatly done child's bonnet which hung almost completed from them.

'I didn't know you went in for this sort of thing, Julie gal,' grinned Ma, knowing the reason for the girl's confusion. A hard-bitten young woman like Julie did not like the idea of anyone knowing knitting was her hobby.

The searching took some time and Caroline sat on her bed for she could not leave the room. She remembered the letter and took it from her vanity bag. Tearing open the flap she pulled out the folded sheets of paper, spread them out and began to read.

'Report of Operative 281 into the killing of Charles William Ford in Lawson, Texas,' she read.

Caroline's eyes went down the printed lines. The report was by the Pinkerton Detective Agency, one she asked for. Up until a few days before Caroline had almost believed her aunt to be right in the crusade against the Democrats. She was preparing a manuscript in her aunt's defence and wrote to ask Pinkertons to uncover the full facts about her uncle's killing. This report told of the findings. Pinkerton's men were very thorough. Caroline saw how thorough as she read. Her face lost some of its colour and her hands shook as she folded the paper and put it into the envelope once more.

'Now you know what it's like, Caroline,' Julie said, dropping down on the bed beside her, dressed and waiting for Bertha to be searched.

'What do you mean?' Caroline replied, clearing her head by an effort.

'Getting searched.'

'Have you done it before?' asked Caroline, although at the moment she did not feel like talking. Her brain felt numb, the news came so brutally frank and she could not do other than believe it to be true. Pinkertons might have their faults but they were efficient and accurate in their findings.

'Done it before,' laughed Julie. 'Every time some influential drunk loses his wallet every gal in the place gets searched. The great seizer, the town marshal to you, comes and hauls the girls down to the jail and his wife, or one of the good ladies of the town searches them. Never find anything but it shows they've tried.'

'But don't you object?'

'No. I don't like it, but that's one of the things like hotel food, managers who skip without paying the cast and hearing folks cheering you that go to make up being on the stage. If we object, the place gets closed and the folks who work in it are looking for a new town.'

In the bar-room Waco carried on with his search. He dis-

48

covered the reason for Wilson's objection to being searched, other than personal hatred. One small case, when opened, proved to contain several articles with which Waco had some knowledge.

First was a mechanical card hold-out, a device used by crooked gamblers to keep a few chosen cards concealed up a sleeve, yet which would, on the pressure being applied to a catch, deliver the cards to the hand, propelled by an arrangement of small springs. The three decks of cards in the box had interesting improvements as Waco found on opening the boxes and examining them. The first deck's backs had small portions of the design shaded out, telling one who knew the code the value of the card and its suit. The shading had been very well done and it took keen eyes to see the difference. Forty-eight of the next deck's cards had been filed down a minute fraction of an inch. The remaining four cards, aces Waco guessed, had only the corners filed down, leaving a slight bulge in the centre. A man needed delicate fingers to feel the bulge but it was there. Take the cards firmly, place them edge down on a table and tap the top, then draw it through the fingers and the four bulged cards stuck, coming out to be used for whatever purpose the owner of the deck wished. The last deck showed to have slick aces, the ace cards' backs being treated with wax and polished so they would slide when given a gentle push, making the cutting of an ace certain for a man who knew the deck's secret. The dice in the case looked all right and Waco did not test them, but he would have taken money they were loaded, had one face filed down slightly or were otherwise treated to improve on Wilson's chances in a game.

'Are you a syndicate man?' Waco asked the sullen gambler as he closed the case and laid it aside.

'No,' came the growling reply.

'Now that's a real pity. I'd like to get a syndicate man with this sort of gear on him. That coach keeps going out of Arizona Territory. Stay with it, we've more than enough crooked gamblers and can spare one or two.'

'Have I any choice?'

'Sure. I'll take you back to the fort and show the soldiers how these decks of cards and sets of dice work. They'll likely laugh themselves dizzy when they see. Now I'll take you, Reverend.'

The gaunt man rose and removed his clothes, laying them on the table. The reason for his sweating so much now became obvious. Under his shirt he wore a thick old red woollen under-

49

shirt, a garment not recommended for travellers in the hot climate of Arizona Territory. Dropping the undershirt on the table Hodges stood back. Waco examined the clothing with no more success than in the previous two cases, then gave his attention to the man's scanty belongings. At the end Waco shrugged. If Mangus Colorado's medicine was on anyone now it must be one of the women.

The preacher dressed and packed his belongings while Waco went to the door of the women's room and knocked.

'Nothing, Ma,' he said when the big woman stepped out.

'Me neither,' she admitted.

Bertha Ford followed Ma from the room, her face flushed with rage. 'I won't forget this outrage!' she almost screamed as she halted before Waco. 'I'll make the whole country ring with the high-handed way you've carried on. I've been forced to suffer the indignity of being searched like a common criminal on baseless suspicion, and without your even knowing what you searched for. I'll take up this matter and break you and your leader—'

'You won't, Aunt Bertha!'

Caroline stepped from the other room, in her hand a thick envelope. She moved by Ma and halted before her aunt.

'What do you mean?' Bertha hissed.

'You're going to stop this senseless attacking of honest men doing their work the only way they can. You're going home, Aunt Bertha, and you're never going near anything political again.'

'Have you taken leave of your senses, girl?'

'No, just come to them,' Caroline replied quietly, but her words seemed to ring through the room. 'Why have you carried on this feud with the Democrats, Aunt Bertha? For your beliefs, or because you hated them for killing Uncle Charles. Which was it Aunt Bertha?'

'I don't know what you mean!'

'Uncle Charles, the noble, generous, kindly reformer. Uncle Charles, Captain of the Texas State Police, protecting the innocent. Murdered by a drunken mob of Democrats,' Caroline went on, her voice throbbing with vibrant passion. 'Uncle Charles was killed by a sheriff whilst resisting arrest on charges of extortion, embezzlement of funds, conspiracy to defraud and accessory before and after the act of murder.'

Bertha Ford's face twisted in a mask of hatred, her eyes glaring in a wild hate-filled mania. 'Be quiet!' she screamed. 'Caroline, I—'

'I won't be quiet,' Caroline answered, holding out the envelope. 'This is the report from the Pinkerton Agency. I asked them to establish the facts of Uncle Charles' death and they told me all about dear, kind, noble Uncle Charles. That's the man who you were prepared to break honest people for, not because of their political beliefs, but because one killed your husband.'

Bertha Ford lunged forward, hands clawing wildly and such an expression of hate on her face that Caroline staggered back.

'Give me that report! Give it to me!'

Ma Randle's big hands shot out to catch Bertha's wrists, holding them with no more effort than one would a child's. She forced the screaming, struggling woman back and thrust her into a chair. For a moment Bertha Ford screamed, raved and tried in vain to shake the hands from her. Then she went limp, slumped in the chair and started to sob, the sobs shaking her frame. Caroline moved forward, face white and set as she looked down at her aunt.

'I'm sorry, Aunt Bertha,' she said gently, 'I'm truly sorry for you. But I'll keep this report and I promise that the next time you attack a Democrat or anyone I'll send it to a newspaper.'

It was the end of Bertha Ford's career of hatred, lies and trouble-making. She knew it as did every man and woman in the room.

Waco spoke first. 'Nothing of what's been said in this room'll be repeated outside it. The man who mentions it answers to me.'

There came a rumble of agreement from the others. Caroline gave Waco a grateful glance. She was not vindictive and knew her aunt had been punished enough. Bertha Ford's power had been broken from the moment the report came into Caroline's hands. If the report ever did reach the Democrat Press her aunt would know in full the bitter taste of her own medicine. Somehow Caroline did not think any of the others would mention the matter after Waco's warning.

Waco's eyes went to the sobbing woman, then at the gaunt reverend who sat at a table so close to her. The man did not appear to be over-interested in anything he had heard or seen. He must be the sort of churchman who held that his services only worked with payment. Then the young Texan turned his mind back to the problem which brought him to Randle's Way Station. A half-forgotten fact nagged at his brain, fought to make the surface and allow light to fall upon it. His eyes went to the leather-bound bible and he remembered he had not examined it. Waco was a man with strong, if not orthodox religious principles and left the bible because he did not feel he should touch the sacred book without something stronger than mere suspicion. Perhaps Mosehan's information had been false and the people on the stage, did not have the medicine. The guilty party might even have made a parcel of the medicine and left it to be delivered east by the United States mail. If that proved to be the case the people would be in a bad spot come daylight.

'Did you ever see Mangus Colorado, Ma?' he asked.

'Old Red Sleeves,' Ma replied, moving back from Bertha. 'Sure I saw him. A big, fine looking man, tall and heavy built. I saw him when—'

The words rolled on but Waco no longer heard them. What a blind fool he'd been not to see it at once. Red Sleeves, the English translation of Mangus Colorado.

The preacher came to his feet in a fast move. His right hand knocked open the bible's cover and dipped into a cavity made by sticking the pages together and cutting the centre away. A Remington Double Derringer came into his hand as he lunged forward.

Bertha Ford gave a startled cry as the man's left hand caught her wrist. He gave a pull and she came to her feet, dragged before him by a strength which was out of keeping with his gaunt frame. She stood between Hodges and the others, a living shield, the Remington thrust into her side and the hammer back ready to fire the upper barrel.

'Stand still, all of you!' he snapped.

Waco's hand froze inches from his guns. Like all the others he had been taken by surprise. The rest stood fast. Ma was first to get it although she was not sure how Hodges tied into the matter. Then she saw the red strip showing from the cuff of the gaunt man's coat, recognized it for what it was.

Mangus Colorado's name came from a red undershirt bought, or looted, from the first American traders to enter the Apache lands. He wore it in battle and came through without a scratch. So it became his medicine, treasured for the luck it brought. When he became an old-man chief and no longer needed to take the risks a name-making brave must, he hung the medicine shirt in the trophy lodge.

The pieces of the puzzle clicked into place like a well-trained troop of cavalry falling into line. Ma saw, as had Waco a few seconds earlier, the meaning of the undershirt worn by Hodges. No man need wear such a thick garment in the heat of the

Arizon Territory; and yet what better way to hide the medicine than to wear it?

'You can't get away with it,' Waco warned.

'I'll take my chances on it,' Hodges replied. 'Throw all the guns behind the bar. Do it easy, Ranger. I couldn't miss at this range.'

Held firmly before the man, Bertha Ford stared at Waco with horror-filled eyes. It suddenly came to her that her life hung in the hands of a man who had no cause to care whether she lived or died. Her fate hung in the balance and at the other end of the scales were two men with good cause to hate her. The young Ranger whom she had accused of murder if nothing worse. The Apache Scout, a member of a force which, according to her, lived for nothing but taking life, torturing innocent and harmless Indians. She wanted to beg them not to move, to obey this man who held her, but the words would not come.

Waco stood perfectly still, watching every move. He needed time to break the deadlock without getting Bertha Ford killed. Waco knew a professional killer when he saw one in action and Hodges gave every sign of being one. There could be no taking rash chances with such a man.

From outside came the call of an owl followed by the shrill yip of a coyote.

'Do as he says,' Waco ordered.

The men obeyed, laying the guns on the top of the bar. Wilson gave a snarl and lunged forward to grab at the driver's old Army Colt, meaning to prove to the women he could handle Hodges. The Remington came round and spat, then went back before Waco, fast as he was, could chance drawing and throwing down on the small target Hodges offered from behind Bertha. Fast though the move was it served. Wilson jerked, his hand missed the gun butt, clutched convulsively at the bar top, then went down in the boned-appearing way of a man head-shot.

'Keep your hands raised high, Ranger,' Hodges warned. 'You're too fast for me to take chances with. Take his gun-belt and the Merwin gun, Miss Clover, and put them behind the bar.'

'Go to h—,' Julie began.

'Do it, gal!' Waco ordered, his voice hard and urgent.

Julie came forward, coming between Waco and the gaunt man. Waco lifted his hands well clear from his sides to show they were not touching anything dangerous and he did not aim

53

to make any wrong moves. Julie unbuckled the belt, then took the Merwin & Hulbert revolver from his waistband.

'Take a chance, Waco,' she whispered.

'He'd shoot through you, or cut her down,' Waco replied no louder. 'Put them over the bar like he says.'

Julie took the gunbelt and lowered it over the bar, following it with the short-barrelled revolver. All the time she was doing this Hodges backed towards the door dragging the terrified woman with him, keeping her as a living shield. Julie's eyes went to Wilson, but one glance told her he was beyond help. A Remington Double Derringer did not have great range, but across the width of the room could carry enough power to kill instantly when its ball struck the head.

'You're in a hell of a state, Mrs. Ford,' Hodges said gently. 'One move from them and I'll down you. If I was that young Ranger I'd make the move. Only he won't. He's not like me. I'm not worried over you but he wants to keep you alive, even if it means getting killed himself. Try thinking about that the next time you want to talk about cold-blooded, murdering lawmen.'

Slowly the man moved. He was by the door and ordered the men to get down on their faces. 'You, too, Ma. You're too handy for me to take chances.'

'Give it up, mister,' Waco put in, obeying the order. 'The place's surrounded and you can't get out.'

'Good try, Ranger,' grinned Hodges. 'You almost sound convincing. I'm taking the horses from the corral. I'll leave you afoot, likely there'll be men out from Mecate when the stage doesn't show.'

'Don't go out there!' Waco warned. 'I'm telling you the place's surrounded.'

Hodges laughed. He thrust the woman away from him, jerked open the door and went through it, slamming it behind him. They heard his footsteps and all the men but Waco came up fast, heading for the bar and their weapons.

'Kill him!' screamed Bertha Ford, defender of the underdog and humanitarian, 'Kill him!'

Waco came to his feet. He heard Hodges' startled yell, the crack of the Remington followed by the bark of a rifle, a scream, then silence until hooves thundered in the darkness and an Apache war yell rang out.

'Like I said,' Waco drawled as he took his gunbelt from Pa who had gone behind the bar and was handing out the weapons. 'I played them close to the vest. There's narry a hoss left in the corral and the place has been surrounded by Apaches ever since the coach pulled in.'

The sun hung just over the horizon at dawn. Before the Way Station Pedro and the other peons returned as mysteriously and silently as they left and hitched a team to the stagecoach. Every horse had been returned just as silently during the night.

Only one passenger's baggage had been loaded on the coach roof. Bertha Ford turned to her niece and asked:

'Won't you come with me?'

'No, Aunt Bertha, I'm going to Texas with Cody and Julie. We're going to see Ysaleta then Julie and I plan to open a dress and hat shop in Dallas or one of the other big towns. Good-bye, Aunt Bertha.'

The woman was at the coach before she spoke again. She looked over her shoulder and asked: 'About the report from the Pinkertons?'

'I won't use it unless I have to.'

With that Caroline turned and entered the Way Station while her aunt climbed into the coach to start her lonely journey east.*

Waco stood by Ma Randle watching the stage pull out. One of the horses belonging to the dead outlaws stood saddled ready for him to ride it back to Albion City instead of waiting another day for a coach.

'I'll never forget last night,' Ma remarked. 'What do you make of it?'

'Reckon we'll never know for sure how or why Hodges took it. What happened after he went through the door's anybody's guess. I hope he was dead when they got him. Maybe one day I'll look up Johnny No-Legs and ask him about it.'

'I meant about that Ford dame,' Ma said.

'Her? She's done now. Miss Caroline burned the report last night after she went to bed but she doesn't know. Don't reckon we'll be bothered by her again. Well, I'll see you, Ma.'

With that Waco stepped from the porch and unfastened the horse. He swung into the saddle, raised his hands in a cheery salute to the two young women and the tall Apache Scout who stepped from the building to join Ma.

The time was long gone for Waco to ride. The Apaches would be content now they'd recovered the medicine so would make no more trouble for Waco. Captain Bertram H. Mosehan would make trouble and plenty of it happen he heard one of his men wasted time in reporting in after finishing a simple job.

* The end of Bertha Ford's story is told in GUNS IN THE NIGHT.

55

CHAPTER TWO

THE JUGGLER AND THE LADY

WACO and his partner, Doc Leroy, entered the stage entrance of the Bella Union Theatre in Bisbee. The old doorkeeper, who should have kept them out, grinned and stood back for he recognized them as the two Arizona Rangers who broke up a tough bunch of crooked gamblers operating in town. They stood in the corridor by the door, looking around at the hustle and bustle of show people preparing to go home for the night. A pair of pretty young women eyed the two Rangers in passing but received no encouragement so passed out into the darkness.

'Waco,' a voice yelled.

A tall, slim man dressed in a good eastern style suit, white shirt and large bow tie of the latest eastern mode, came from a dressing-room. He advanced with hand held out and a broad smile on his face.

'Waco, it's good to see you. How are you, boy?'

'Fit as a flea and twice as lively,' Waco replied, taking the hand. 'Elwin, you sure look elegant. Don't reckon you know my partner, Doc Leroy?'

The slim man held out his hand to Doc Leroy. They were much alike in size and build, not as tall as Waco and slimmer. Yet Doc Leroy looked as much a Texas cowhand as did his young partner. There was a pallor about Doc's face, but he had the sort of skin which would never tan, not the pallor of indoor life. He wore a low-crowned black Stetson hat, a bandana tight rolled and knotted at his throat, an open-necked green shirt. The collar was over the collar of his jacket and the jacket's side stitched back to leave clear the ivory butt of his Colt Civilian Peacemaker. The Colt hung in a holster like the kind Waco wore, the holder of a real fast man with a gun.

Doc Leroy could claim to be real fast with a gun. Once he rode as a member of the Wedge crew of trail-driving cowhands, taking herds from Texas to Kansas railheads. When the drives ended and Stone Hart took a ranch Doc went to the Rio Hondo to join Ole Devil Hardin's OD Connected ranch as Waco's sidekick. They had been cowhands together, now they rode as Arizona Rangers. Doc gained his name through two years spent in an eastern hospital. He hoped to qualify as a doctor but force of circumstances sent him west.* He carried on his learning as best he could, reading medical books, working with doctors in towns that housed him for any time or by experience gained through being the only one with any knowledge among the cowhands. He could set broken bones, diagnose and advise the treatment of most illnesses he came across and knew more about bullet extraction than the average eastern doctor learned in a lifetime. A couple of yeard older than Waco, Doc brought a steadying influence his friend often needed.

'Enjoyed your act in there, Elwin,' Doc drawled.

Elwin accepted the praise with the polished charm of a top-grade performer. He had done well in his profession since starting out after the siege at Baptist's Hollow,† where he first met Waco. Now Elwin was one of the best known jugglers in the West and his act much in demand in all the better class houses.

'Thanks,' he said. 'Pleased to meet you, Doc. Are you working?'

'Hush now, friend,' warned Doc. 'You'll give the boy the vapours saying a word like that.'

'Sure,' agreed Waco, accepting that to Doc and all his friends he was a boy still. 'We're hiding. Just ended a chore and hoping that mean ole Cap'n Mosehan don't get word to us until Monday. How's Janice?'

Elwin looked slightly disturbed at the mention of his wife, 'She's all right. We're staying at the Creed Hotel. She reckons we can't afford the Bisbee Grand yet.'

'She's not singing now?' Waco went on. The last time he had seen Elwin and his wife they were working as a team and she also appeared as a single act, singing nostalgic songs which went down well among the hard-rock miners and cowhands in the audience.

'Not at the moment,' Elwin replied; a trifle evasively Waco thought: 'It wouldn't be fitting with Lily Carlisle on the same bill.'

* Told in THE TOWN TAMERS.
† Told in APACHE RAMPAGE.

'Elwin, darling!'

The juggler jerked around in a rather guilty manner, threw a glance at the stage door, then looked towards the woman who came towards him.

Lily Carlisle never approached like an ordinary woman; she descended, swooping down in all her majesty as became a great star and a lady of some quality in the theatre. On her head was a huge hat with ostrich plumes bowing and showing her glistening black hair to its best advantage. The face had great beauty, the theatrical make-up enhancing it. Yet her dark eyes had an imperious look about them and her mouth, held in a gracious smile, did not look a happy mouth. She stood at least five foot eight and her figure, rich and full, set off the skin-tight bosom and waist of her deep blue dress.

Behind Lilly came the two tall, muscular young men who assisted her in her act. They wore evening dress now, not the leopard skin leotards and white tights of professional strong men. Yet they looked the same, two young *galants* with muscles and all their brains in their faces. Tagging along in the rear, eyes adoringly devouring the great woman, came a tall, good-looking young man with the badge of a deputy marshal of Bisbee's police force on his vest. He moved by the party as it halted, making for the door that he might open it and be given a smile, perhaps even a word of thanks from Lily Carlisle.

'Lily,' Elwin said, his voice polite as became a juvenile when addressing one of the greats of their mutual world, 'I'd like to present two good friends, Waco and Doc Leroy.'

'Good evening,' Lily Carlisle replied, icily distant. 'Come now, Elwin. I've ordered a meal to be waiting in my rooms.' Taking the juggler's arm she led him to the door, the other two men following like a pair of well-trained beagles. 'You really must think about your act, dear boy. How can you ever expect to get anywhere with that corny routine?'

Elwin tried to speak, to turn and make an apology to Waco and Doc for his sudden departure, but he was borne off by the woman, her words coming loud and drowning him. He wanted to get away but was afraid any slight might cause Lily to have his act cancelled. She was the star of the show and Elwin knew he could not claim to have anywhere near her standing. He needed the work, more so in view of circumstances as they stood at the moment. One word from Lily might blast his career, or so he thought.

The young deputy pulled open the door, his hat in his free hand, a look of rapture on his face. Lily favoured him with a smile and passed through with the juggler carried along in her reflected glory.

'He sure was pleased to see you,' drawled Doc, for Waco spoke of Elwin as an old friend.

'Likely didn't have any choice at all,' Waco replied. 'He's a big man in the theatre now and she's one of the tophands. Anyways, you'd've gone just as easy with her.'

'Not me. I like mine smaller, with less heft and some better tempered.'

Which proved Doc to be as keen-eyed and observant as his partner and just as capable of summing up a character.

Exchanging grins the two Rangers walked to the door. The young deputy leaned against it, a blissful smile on his face. He did not offer to open the door for the two Texans. Waco and Doc passed out of the theatre into the night air and halted on the sidewalk.

'What now?' asked Doc. 'Feel like a beer, or shall we head for the hotel?'

'I'd as soon go to bed,' Waco replied. 'Sure hope Bisbee livens up tomorrow. We could've had as much fun heading for Prescott.'

Creed's Hotel stood on Jack Street, once the pride of Bisbee but now dwarfed and rendered insignificant by the larger and more modern Grant Hotel which stood a couple of blocks farther down the street. However the Creed still drew in a good class of client, not the rich miners and their kind who once thronged the reception hall and drank at the bar, but still a good class of people.

Looking up from his desk the night-clerk handed Waco a room key and the two Texans went upstairs. He watched them go with an admiring stare for he was one who profited by their smashing the crooked gambling ring.

Waco and Doc walked along the passage to their room and the young Texan placed the key into its keyhole. A door behind them opened and a young woman leaned against the jamb, staring at them.

'Help me—!' she gasped.

Turning Waco sprang forward but Doc beat him to it, catching the girl and taking her back into the room. Waco followed, watching the gentle way his partner eased the girl down on to the bed. The young Texan went closer, hardly able to believe his eyes for he knew the girl, Janice Greener, wife of Elwin the Juggler, had always been a plump young thing but there now was a fattening about her middle which spelled only one thing. Her hair hung lank and dead looking and her face was without make-up.

'What is it, Janice?' he asked.

'Waco!' Janice replied, her pain-filled eyes recognizing him. 'I'm starting, I think. Wh—where's Elwin?'

Bending over Janice, Doc took her wrist between his forefinger and thumb. He did not need telling what ailed the girl. He looked at Waco after taking Janice's pulse, his voice low and gentle.

'Go get a doctor, boy!'

'I want Elwin,' gasped Janice. 'Where is he?'

'Lay easy, gal, lay easy,' drawled Doc gently but there was no gentleness in his eyes and voice as he looked at Waco. 'Get the hell out of here. Shake the bull-droppings from your socks, boy!'

Waco turned and headed for the door. Doc's temper was uncertain when faced with a doctoring chore. The young Texan felt some relief to see a woman, dressed in a coat thrown over a night gown, standing at the door. He opened his mouth but Doc beat him to it.

'This gal's going to have a baby real soon, ma'am,' he said. 'Move, boy!'

Heading downstairs three at a time Waco felt scared. Janice had been a healthy, happy girl the last time he saw her, not that weeping, frightened thing lying on the bed.

'Where'd I find a doctor?' he asked the clerk.

'You don't tonight, Ranger. Both doctors went out of town earlier, to a mine accident and won't be back until tomorrow noon at best.'

Waco flung himself distractedly up the stairs and gave the news to Doc. He came back down to the desk in less than three minutes, thrusting a sheet of paper under the clerk's nose.

'Here, take this to the doctor's house. Show it his wife, if he's got one. Tell whoever's there to bring this gear, *pronto*.'

'I ain't supposed to leave the desk,' the clerk replied. 'What's wrong?'

'Gal going to have a baby,' Waco answered. 'You know Bisbee better than I do. I'll watch the desk while you go.'

The clerk argued no more. He took the paper, looking uncomprehendingly at the scribbled words, then left the hotel at a dead run.

Pacing the floor Waco looked like a great nervous cat. Never had he been so close to a woman in the supreme moment of childbirth and the feeling scared him. He was frightened and worried, not by doubts that Doc couldn't handle the birth, but with a bachelor's fear of the unknown mystery of that great thing, the birth of a child.

Minutes dragged by and the clerk entered with a woman who carried a doctor's bag in her hands. The woman who had entered the upstairs room came into sight at the stairhead and yelled:

'Where's the doctor?'

'Out on a call,' replied the doctor's wife. 'How about the one who sent that list for me?'

'He's a cowhand—'

'Anyone who can make out a list the way he did can do all that needs doing, I reckon. Who sent it?'

'My partner, Doc Leroy, ma'am,' Waco replied. 'He's the Arizona Ranger who broke the typhoid outbreak in Canvastown last year.'

'I'll get on up then, he can handle this.'

Before the woman could move towards the stairs Doc appeared at the top and his irate bellow came down: 'Waco! Where in hell's name's that gear I sent for.'

'He sounds just like my husband,' the doctor's wife remarked and strode forward in the purposeful manner of one long used to dealing with this sort of situation.

Doc met her halfway up the stairs, listened to her explanation and saw he must handle the confinement himself. His temper, never too certain with outsiders when handling medical work, evened a little for he knew the doctor's wife would be a great help to him.

'Waco,' Doc called, as he turned. 'The gal wants her husband. She won't rest easy until he comes. Go get him.'

Waco turned and left hurriedly. The cool night wind, even tainted by the smells of what he regarded as a big city, calmed him. He stood for a moment on the sidewalk, thinking of where he could find Elwin. There could only be one place. He had left the theatre to have a meal with Lily Carlisle in her room and a star of her magnitude must room at the Grand Hotel.

So Waco headed for the elegant portals of the hotel. He passed through the door, crossing the ankle-deep carpet and halted by the desk. The clerk of the Grand was a different type to the Creed's man. He wore a neat suit and his cravat looked tight enough to choke him. Raising a supercilious eye the clerk studied the young Texan, then looked down once more at the newspaper before him.

Two hands slapped down hard on the paper. The clerk

looked up to meet a pair of blue eyes which were cold and threatening as the full blast of a Texas blue-norther storm.

'Miss Carlisle's room,' Waco said quietly.

'Why?' purred the clerk, recovering his aplomb and preparing to handle a familiar situation.

Waco did not waste time. His hands shot up, bunching the clerk's lapels and hauling him halfway across the desk. Thrusting his face up close, Waco growled, 'I said where's Miss Carlisle's room?'

Then he thrust the man back again, realizing strong arm tactics would only cause delay. He slid his hand to a concealed pocket under his shirt and brought out a card which he laid on the desk. The man glanced down, looked again hard and gave a gulp of surprise.

'Yes sir,' he gasped, watching the Ranger's identification card disappear again. No man in Arizona Territory liked to cross one of Mosehan's boys. 'First floor, the suite facing the stair-head.'

Striding up the stairs Waco looked along the empty passage. The Grand had rooms to spare on the first floor and only one showed signs of life. Waco crossed to this door and knocked; one of the muscular young men looked out from a two-inch crack.

'I'd like to see Elwin,' said Waco politely.

'Sorry, cowboy, we don't want any.'

With that the man closed the door again. At the well set table Elwin looked around. He had heard the voice and recognized it, guessing what brought Waco after him and wanting to leave. Yet Lily had been a gracious hostess, champagne flowed freely and she appeared to be taking a genuine interest in improving his act. He started to push back his chair as Philip closed the door while Harry, the other strong man member of Lily's act, opened a further bottle of champagne. Lily glanced at the door, making an annoyed gesture.

There sounded a crash and the door burst open. Waco stepped inside fast, his kick had been delivered with precision and in a manner learned in more dangerous conditions than these.

'Elwin,' he said, ignoring the others. 'You'd best get back to Janice, it's near her time.'

Even as Elwin pushed back his chair, Lily Carlisle came to her feet, pointing at Waco, her voice a hag-ridden screech. 'Throw that bum out!'

Phil stepped forward, arms spread, meaning to encircle

Waco from behind and hold him while Harry worked him over. They had operated the same trick before on cowhands. Only Waco was no cowhand. He had learned frontier brawling under a good master and was fully capable of handling the situation.

Driving back hard Waco's elbow smashed into Phil's body just under his breast bone. The big man let out a croak of agony and stumbled back, hitting the wall, holding his body as he doubled over in pain.

Throwing himself into a pugilistic posture Harry started forward but came to a sudden halt. Waco's left hand dipped and brought out the staghorn butted Colt from its holster lining it and drawing back the hammer with an audible click.

'Hold it, *hombre*!' he barked. 'I've no time for fussing, Elwin, that gal wants you. Do you walk or get carried?'

Elwin came to his feet, head spinning with the effects of the champagne but he could still think for himself. He looked at Lily, seeing the anger on her face but more concerned about his wife's well-being.

'It's Jan, Lily,' he said. 'I told you we were expecting a baby. I'll have to go to her.'

Watching the woman Waco could never remember when he saw so much concentrated fury and hatred on a face. He moved back so he could watch both the muscle-men for Phil had made his feet and stood scowling at him.

'I'm sorry to bust your party up, ma'am,' Waco said. 'It wouldn't look too good for either of you happen word got out Elwin was here with you when his wife needed him.'

Saying that Waco holstered his Colt. He had given Lily the one argument which would make her see reason. All too well did Lily Carlisle know the value of newspaper publicity. She also knew nothing would ruin her image quicker than having it said Elwin was with her at a time when he should have been with his wife.

She watched the door close, then snatched up a bottle and hurled it across the room to shatter on the wall by Phil's head.

'A lot of good you were!' she screamed as the man ducked to avoid the flying splinters of glass. 'I had him eating out of my hand. I could have made him change his act and ruined him. But you two had to let that damned cowhand take him out of the room. Get out of my sight, both of you!'

The men slunk from Lily's presence like cur-dogs after a whipping. She stood at the table, her beautiful face twisted into an expression of rage and her hands clenched into fists.

Suddenly the beauty had all gone, leaving only a vicious, shrewish virago who felt the touch of age upon her. She hated Elwin's youth, his popularity with the audiences. She hated the fact that he gained more applause than she did, that his act attracted more customers than did her own. Lily Carlisle, once the top of her profession, the darling of two continents, now played a circuit of western towns. True she only played the biggest and best houses but no longer did New York, London, Paris clamour for her. A trip like this, knowing an unknown was topping her act on the stage, if not in billing, could ruin her. For that reason and no other she lavished charm and attention on the young juggler, preparing to ruin him, spoil his popularity.

Now there would be no chance. Elwin was a good husband and would be too engrossed in his new family to fall for dinner engagements. In her rage Lily gripped the tablecloth and tore it from the table, sending the dinner service, glasses and bottles smashing to the floor.

Waco and Elwin walked from the hotel and along the sidewalk. The juggler looked at the grim-faced young Texan.

'Is she all right?'

'Doc's with her,' growled Waco. 'If you care.'

'Lord what a fool I've been,' Elwin groaned, ignoring the last words. 'I ought to have gone straight to her after my act. I should have—'

'Don't cry on my shoulder. You're a man grown and likely to be a father come morning.'

'You don't understand,' Elwin replied. 'Lily Carlisle's big, she's a star. She's topping the bill in the big time and could see my right—'

'Way I see it you're doing all right,' Waco interrupted. 'Considering two years ago you were selling dishes in a general store. I saw you when you headed the bill in Tombstone.'

'Tombstone—'

'Don't sell it short. Cap'n Bert took me backstage one time to meet Eddie Foy, he reckons to be big on the stage. He was leading at Tombstone and reckoned it was one of the top-grade houses.'

The discussion ended there for they had reached the Creed Hotel and Elwin darted upstairs fast. Waco followed at a more leisurely pace, halting by the closed door and listening to the low mumble of voices. He handrolled a cigarette, lit it then drew in the smoke.

Time dragged by, then the door opened. Doc came out

followed by Elwin who stared back in a distracted manner towards the bed. Doc eased him out and closed the door gently.

'This's going to take longer than I thought,' Doc remarked with the casual ease of one who had seen and done it all before. 'Don't you worry none. I never lost a father, mother or child yet and this's my fourth try. You'd best bunk down with Waco for the night and don't bother us in there. We'll tell you soon enough when it's over.'

With that gentle warning Doc turned on his heel to enter the room and close the door again. Elwin stared at it, taking a step forward but Waco caught him by the arm and held him.

'You go in there and ole Doc's like to pitch you through the window, which same he's the only doctor in town so that'll make him more work and he won't be fit to talk with for a week.'

Elwin stared at Waco in the distracted manner of every father while waiting for the arrival of his first born. Waco could see sleep would not come to Elwin so suggested they took a walk.

The streets of Bisbee were quiet and almost deserted. Only a few lights remained glowing and few places were open. Waco saw a small saloon still open and steered Elwin into it, putting him at a table and crossing to the bar.

'Two beers, colonel, and take something yourself,' he said.

'You or him?' asked the bartender, pouring the drinks.

'That went right by me,' Waco drawled. 'I never saw it at all.'

'Who's the father?' grinned the bartender. 'I've seen the sign too often not to know it.'

'Elwin is,' grinned Waco. 'Do I look like the marrying kind?'

'None of us do – until we're caught, stretched and hung on the wall.'

'We're not keeping you open are we?' asked Waco, seeing only one other customer, a tallish, wizened old man who sat in a corner nursing an empty glass and muttering to himself in the manner of one long drunk.

'Nope, the boss wants the place keeping open in case any trade comes in. I get paid and don't have more'n a lick of work to do, so why should I beef about it.'

Waco took the two glasses across the room, sat at Elwin's table and the bartender followed. He was bored, could see Elwin needed the confidence of a man who knew what the first child meant.

The man in the corner of the room came to his feet. He stared around in the bemused manner of a drunk, then started forward on unsteady feet towards the door. However before he reached the batwings he stopped, peering towards the three men at the table. He changed direction and headed for the table.

Studying the man, as he always studied anyone who came towards him, Waco made a quick assessment of his character. Tall, with bowed shoulders, a parchment-like face, the skin white with an unhealthy pallor, a face which might once have shown some character, not handsome perhaps but strong and virile. It was the sort of face which might slide fast if once it lost its grip. The man's thinning white hair shed dandruff on to his threadbare black coat. His shirt might have been clean the day the Appomattox Court House saw the end of the Civil War, but had not been washed since from the look of it. He wore patched and threadbare trousers, scarred and dirty shoes which looked too large for him. His hands caught Waco's eye, in fact being the first thing at which the young Texan looked. The hands were grimy, dirt ingrained into them and with filthy long finger-nails, yet they were long, thin and restless hands. To Waco's eyes those hands had once been dexterous and fast; the kind of hands which could manipulate a deck of cards, play a piano or maybe even throw shots from a real fast drawn Colt. Such hands had Doc Leroy and he had skill in all those matters.

'So, my young friend,' the old man said, leaning forward on to the table and peering owlishly down at Elwin. 'You have escaped from the cave of Circe without being turned into a swine.'

The men at the table looked up, Waco frowned. 'Who's this Circe?'

'Don't ask me,' Elwin answered.

'Circe, daughter of Helios,' put in the bartender. 'Some Greek gal used to turn men into animals. Had an old pianner player used to come here and was always telling me things about them Greeks, right lively crowd they looked to be.'

'You escaped from her net, young man,' the old drunk muttered, swaying on the table. 'How did you slip from her mesh?'

'If I knew who you were talking about I might explain,' Elwin answered with a smile. 'Does Lily know you're in here and drunk like this?'

Leaning forward the old man's eyes fixed on Elwin. 'Lily,

66

the incomparable Lily. Circe with her potions ready to destroy men. And you are to be destroyed, my boy. You are to be destroyed.'

Elwin shoved back his chair, glancing at Waco, then giving the old man his attention. 'I reckon you'd better get back to the theatre and sleep it off, Reuben,' he said.

'Hold hard, let him set and take a drink,' Waco interrupted.

'A drink?' The old man sank into a chair, his body smelling of whisky and dry sweat. 'You, sir, are a gentleman of some taste and refinement. Had I not, inadvertently, left my wallet in my dressing-room I would never permit you to pay.'

'You've landed a good one here, friend,' said the bartender, with a knowledge of drunken moochers behind him.

'Get him a drink, will you,' Waco replied.

Taking a pull which all but emptied the four-finger whisky glass the old man sank back in his chair.

'You are a strong man, sir,' he told Waco with drunken gravity. 'A man of prompt action and some strength of character. I was such a man when your age. A man of some ability. So also was the Great Rube, the Tramp Magician. I will tell you of the Great Rube and hope the parable of his sad tale will serve to save another from going his way.'

Catching Waco's nod the bartender poured the old man another drink, then sat down. Serving drinks throughout the West had made the bartender something of a student of men and his every instinct told him the old drunk might have an interesting story to tell. If not all the bartender wasted was his time and he would get paid for the same time anyhow.

'The Great Rube,' the old man sighed out the words. 'There was a name to conjure with, my friends. You won't have heard of him. He never played the hinterland, only the best of eastern houses. He performed feats of prestidigitation which held audiences spellbound. Do you know he could take an ordinary, unprepared deck of cards and cut any number called for by the audience and also cut any card named.'

Waco, no mean hand with cards, thought of all the gamblers he had known, men who could perform feats that would baffle a stage sleight-of-hand showman, but not one of them could perform the tricks the old man spoke of.

'Now this Great Rube was a man with a roaming eye for the ladies, a gallant with a flair for attracting the beauties of his day. Quite a fine figure of a man, except when on the stage. There, well, magnificent is too small a word. He had a genius all of his own. He could evoke laughter and sympathy as the ragged and unkempt clown. So the audiences loved him, his act stood at the top of the bill, a place no other sleight-of-hand man ever attained. And he met a girl. A beautiful girl. He found her singing in an obscure bar in New York, a waif with a beautiful face. He took her from that drab setting and brought her into his own act. Then started her on her own, having her voice trained by a European master. Soon she rose up the scale, taking her place on the bill beneath his own. They toured the world, playing the best houses and all the time this girl kept at the Great Rube to change his act. It was undignified, she told him. He should throw off the tramp's rags and show himself as a true performer.'

Here the old man paused and replenished his glass. The bartender sat back and watched the other men. He recognized both Elwin and Waco, wondering what strange circumstances brought the young juggler and the tough young Arizona Ranger together. He also mused the strange ways of men, which led the three of them to sit in the bar at midnight, listening to the mutterings of a drunken old man.

'So, gentlemen, where was I?' the man went on. 'I remember. The Great Rube took the girl's advice. He shed his tramp costume and came out on to the stage with his evening suit. And died. The audience did not come to see a man perform card tricks. They came to be entranced by the wizardry of a tramp. He would not admit they could be right and, encouraged by that woman, tried to force them to accept his act. He forgot that a performer is nothing more than a storekeeper, selling his wares. He talked of art, of not wishing to be remembered as nothing but a tramp. He did not sell the public what they wanted and his popularity waned. With the wane came the bottle, the all-night drinking, the mornings after when his hands would no longer obey the dictates of his mind. He fell below his protégé in billing and tried to fight back. She helped him, with kind words, soothed him by talk of the stupidity of the fools who wouldn't see his act was better and consoled him with whisky. So he declined, gentlemen, and she rose higher, dragging the crumbling wreck of the Great Rube behind her, ever sinking him lower until he became—'

Once more the old man paused, taking a drink. Then his head fell on to his hands, the whisky suddenly catching and affecting him. His eyes lifted towards Elwin.

'She has destroyed one man, Elwin the Juggler. Think of that before you listen to the siren song of Circe.'

With that his head fell forward again and a snore rocked

him. Elwin reached out a hand to shake the old man but the bartender shook his head.

'Won't do no good, friend. Who is he?'

'Lily Carlisle's dresser,' Elwin replied. 'She calls him Reuben. What was he on about?'

'Who knows what goes on in the mind of a drunk?' asked the bartender. 'I've had them tell me their life stories by the hundred, some of them even tell two or three different stories.'

'But he wasn't talking about himself.'

'You could be right at that,' Waco drawled. He glanced at the clock and yawned, although he never felt less like sleeping.

'We should be getting back,' Elwin gasped, suddenly recalling how he left his wife.

'Remember when I had my first,' remarked the bartender. 'I was worried near on sick about it for days. Then one night while I was serving bar the doctor came in, asked for four fingers neat then told me to get out the cigars. It was as easy as that—'

'But Jan's delicate—'

'She's strong as a Texas bull-pup,' Waco corrected. 'And you know it.'

For all his light words Waco wondered how Elwin must feel, knowing the woman he loved and married was going through the hell of childbirth and that his own effort caused it. Waco felt a cold touch at his nerves, then relief as he decided it would never happen to him. He surely did not aim to get tangled with any gal, marry her and watch her change until she looked as Janice had, or go through what Elwin was suffering now.

Elwin almost threw the chair over in his eagerness to rise. The two young men made for the door and the bartender cleared away the glasses, cast a look at the sleeping man and walked behind the bar. He leaned his elbows on the polished surface and shook his head.

'I reckon I know who Circe is, old timer,' he mused. 'And who the Great Rube is too.'

At the Creed Hotel Elwin raced upstairs and tapped on his room door. It was opened by the doctor's wife and she stepped out, closing it behind her.

'Is she all right?' Elwin gasped. 'Is she going to be all right, what—'

'Hold hard, son,' replied the woman. 'First off, she's all right. The baby's not here yet, in fact it won't be here until tomorrow most likely.' She paused and held up a hand. 'Now don't go into a tizzy, it's not the first time I've seen it happen, nor likely to be the last.'

'But—but—'

'There's no buts about it,' the woman answered. 'Your wife's all right and that young feller in there knows what he's doing.'

'Can I see her?'

'Not right now. She's sleeping and we don't want her disturbing. You'd best go and have some sleep yourself.'

A powerful hand caught Elwin's arm, turning him and leading him towards the door of Waco's room. The young Texan grinned as he steered Elwin inside.

'You make yourself to home in there,' he ordered.

Elwin thought he would never sleep but his head barely touched the pillow before he was asleep. Waco undressed and turned into the other bed of the room. He lay awake for a time but sleep came at last.

The sound of water splashing woke Waco. He sat up in bed and found Doc washing in the basin by the door. Waco rolled from bed and pulled on his trousers and socks, then crossed and took the soap from Doc.

'Was everything all right?' he asked.

Doc's eyes met Waco's. 'As right as can be expected. That's a tolerable hefty button she's toting. Too big for my liking.'

'You mean there's some danger?'

'Nope, I mean it's not going to be easy on her.'

At that moment Elwin woke and sat up. He bounded from the bed and darted across the room.

'Doc,' he gasped. 'How is she?'

'Sat in there drinking coffee and looking purty as a June bug,' Doc replied. 'And afore you ask, no, she ain't had it, nor likely to until this afternoon. I'll stay on with her unless the town's doctors get back, which from all I hear ain't likely. Let you see her when you're tidied up a mite. Don't want you going in there looking like you been sleeping in your clothes, even if you have.'

A clean shaven, tidy-looking husband was taken in to see his wife. Janice lay in the bed face pale but smiling as she kissed him. The doctor's wife withdrew and left them together. It took some doing but Janice managed to soothe her husband and Elwin left the room feeling ready to deal with the world, to take care of everything and everybody single handed.

He went to the dining-room with Waco and found to his amazement that they'd slept late and soon he would need to appear for the first show at the theatre. He did not mind, the

70

later he arrived the less chance there was of meeting Lily Carlisle and Elwin did not think his company would be welcome
after the previous night.

'I'd sure like to stay and see the show,' Waco remarked as
they left the hotel. 'But I want to see the sheriff on some business for Cap'n Bert.'

'I'll see you after,' Elwin replied.

Never had Elwin given such a performance. He was inspired
and the crowd roared their approval. His juggling was faultless
but the comic patter he filled in with as backing for his act
swelled to heights he had never shown before.

Lily Carlisle sat in her dressing room and listened. At each
fresh outburst of acclaim her hands clenched and her lips grew
tighter. The two young men, dressed in their leopard skin
leotards and tights, stood at the back of the room and waited
for the explosion they knew would surely come. Reuben, the
old dresser moved around, being cursed every time he tried to
help and getting cursed even more if he did nothing.

'How can I go on after that?' she screamed when a particularly loud burst of laughter and applause sounded.

'You could follow anything and top anybody, Lily,' Reuben
replied.

It was the wrong thing to do for it brought her attention to
him. She came to her feet, her hand swung around to slap his
face and spin him across the room.

'I had him!' she screamed. 'Last night I had him eating out
of the palm of my hand. I could have broken him. Now listen.
He's greater than ever.'

A knock came on the door and a youthful voice called, 'One
minute, Miss Carlisle.'

Lily swept by Elwin with her lips drawn into a tight line as
she ignored him and stalked on to the stage to begin her act.
The orchestra in the small pit before the stage gave careful
attention to their following of the music. This was in some
measure a tribute to a great performer but mostly because
Lily's vile temper would be poured out upon the head of the
conductor and any man who dropped a sour note.

For all the fact that Lily was on stage the audience was restless, still laughing and repeating Elwin's better jokes to each
other. It was the situation which often came when a serious
act followed one of comedy, especially a comedy act as brilliant
as Elwin's inspired efforts. Her first number went by with no
great feeling for or against and although the audience quietened
down after it Lily knew they were not solidly behind her,

hanging on to her every note in the manner to which she was accustomed.

Theatres of the West had not yet discarded the old tradition and switched over to the regulated lines of seats which were becoming the fashion in the East. Instead the audience sat around tables of various sizes, or stood along the walls or at the large bar which showed through an alcove, with a fair sized bar-room to it. The stage was large enough to present quality acts with numerous props, the orchestra pit being separated from the audience by a small barricade. In front of this sat the master of ceremonies, who almost always seemed to be large, well dressed and jovial men with booming voices that carried to every corner of the room, a quick wit to make flashing and sometimes crushing replies to comments from the audience, and an ability to consume good quantities of liquid refreshment without it having any visible effect on them.

All this Lily saw as she went through her act mechanically having done it so many times she only found difficulty when she started to think about what she was doing. Rage seethed in her mind, hate consuming her behind that smiling face and the rich tones of her voice. She wanted revenge on the young juggler, to smash him into the ground, to squash him like a bug. Then she would be the star of the bill for no other player on the circuit had that magical quality showed by Elwin and she would reign supreme once more.

A party at a table right up front caught her eye. They did not look the sort of people who would occupy the place of honour in the house, especially a house like the Bisbee Bella Union. Six men and a girl sat at the table, five of the men in cowhand dress, unshaven and hard looking. The sixth man was tall, wide shouldered and handsome in a reckless kind of way. His expensive Stetson hat lay on the table before him, his black hair was short and very curly, while his cheeks were the dark blue of a man with a heavy-growing beard. He wore a gambler's cutaway coat, frilly fronted shirt, light grey trousers. Yet there was no indoor pallor to his skin, his face held a tan of many hours under the sun. Instead of town shoes he wore high heeled, fancy stitched cowhand boots and around his waist was a gun-belt. Once when he moved she saw he had matched ivory handled Colts in the holsters. Clearly he was a man of importance. That showed in his having a front seat and in the way the men with him or seated at the surrounding tables waited for his reaction before showing any sign. If he laughed at Lily's remarks between songs the men around laughed, if he applauded they seemed to try and outdo each other in their efforts to applaud. The party at his table received prompt attention from the waiters who served them with best whisky at the dark haired man's slightest nod.

Lily glanced at the girl who sat by the man. Her tawny hair looked wild and untouched by the hands of a hairdresser. It framed a tanned beautiful face which looked as wild and free as the range country. She wore a light blue shirt-waister which matched her eyes and clung to the rich full swell of her breasts. The top buttons were unfastened, just a trifle lower than might be decorous, showing the valley between her round bosom. The shirt-waister ended tucked into a pair of blue jeans which looked as if she'd been moulded into them, while beaded Indian moccasins graced her feet. Lily felt disturbed as she saw the girl and their eyes met. One thing Lily Carlisle could not stand was another beautiful woman being near her. The chorus girls were bad enough, but to have such a beautiful creature in the audience hit Lily far worse.

The act came to an end almost without Lily being aware of it. She left the stage and then held out her hands for the two young men to lead her back out again. Sinking into a graceful curtsey she acknowledged the applause then returned to the wings.

'Charles,' she hissed, catching sight of the stage-manager as he tried to get away. 'Come here.'

The man drew in a deep breath and walked towards Lily, clearly steeling himself for a succession of complaints. 'Yes, Lily?'

'Who's that man out front, at the best table?'

'They call him Graham.'

Something in the stage manager's tone told Lily he held something back about the man called Graham. Ignoring the bustle as the cast of the show prepared to go out for the finale she hissed:

'Who is he?'

Seeing the sudden anger which flared into Lily's eyes the stage manager gave a nervous gulp. He knew better than try and evade answering a question when Lily looked like that. It would only lead to a scene in the wings or after the show and he didn't feel he could cope with any more of Lily's tantrums.

'His real name's Brocious, they call him Curly Bill.'

Then Lilly remembered. The show had been playing Tombstone a few weeks ago and the man came in, swaggering at the head of a bunch of tough-looking cowhands with guns bouncing on their hips. Up until that night the Earp brothers had been on hand each night to keep order in the theatre and bask in Lily's reflected glory, grabbing some valuable newspaper space in the process. Yet on this night the Earps were conspicuous only by their absence. In fact rumour was strong in the Tombstone bars that a sudden and urgent business called the Earp brothers and their satellites out of town shortly before the arrival of Curly Bill Brocious, Johnny Ringo and their Galeyville rustlers.

Lily also remembered how Curly Bill removed his hat in a low bow to her, apologized for interrupting her act, then ordered everyone in the theatre to enjoy themselves. Never since the days of her greatest fame had her reception been so enthusiastic at the end of an act. Her anger against the latecomers had died a trifle and died even further when she received a diamond bracelet neatly wrapped and accompanied by a note of apology neatly written and perfectly phrased in a manner she found hard to attribute to Curly Bill. Actually the note had been Curly Bill's only in that he placed it with the bracelet he bought. Curly's partner, Johnny Ringo, that coldly mysterious, deadly killer, wrote it for in his past he had been well educated in the social graces.

Snapping her fingers a moment before she made her grand final entrance Lily brought a stagehand to her.

'Go and tell Mr. Graham I will take champagne with him in the bar in fifteen minutes,' she ordered.

The stagehand hurried away to deliver the message. The stage manager and Lily's two young men heard the order and wondered at it. Lily was smiling as she went forward to take Elwin's hand and allowed him, as always, to lead her to the centre of the stage. Behind her the two young men, coming out to take their final bows, exchanged looks. They knew their Lily very well. When her face held that particular smile somebody usually got hurt.

'Elwin,' Lily whispered. 'Come to my dressing room before you go home to your darling little wife. I feel I must make amends to her for last night. I honestly didn't know of her condition.'

Elwin felt as if a weight had been lifted from his head. He wanted to keep in Lily's good graces and thought she might still be offended at his departure the previous night. It seemed that Lily had come through like the good trouper she was.

'Thanks, Lily,' he managed to get out as he took her forward and waved to the audience, keeping them applauding Lily.

Then the curtains closed and Lily moved back. It always took Elwin at least half an hour to remove his make-up, change and pack away his gear. Lily wore her stage dress but it would be more than suitable for meeting Curly Bill Brocious and preparing the ground for Elwin's downfall.

'Ah, my dear Mr. Graham!'

Lily came into the bar-room in all her regal splendour, sweeping down towards the large round table at which Curly Bill and his men sat. Lily frowned as she saw the girl also sat at the table.

Bill came to his feet at the approach of the woman, landing a kick across the shins of the nearest man who, not so well versed in social graces, remained seated. The others all got to their feet, looking embarrassed as shambling, awkward schoolboys as they removed their hats.

'Howdy, Miss Carlisle,' greeted Curly Bill, retaining some of his usual easy familiarity in the presence of greatness. 'You were great today, just great. Wasn't she, Tioga?'

'Yeah,' replied the tawny-haired girl, meeting Lily's eyes without flinching. 'Great.'

The warmth flickered for an instant from Lily's face, her mouth dropped and then the stage smile returned. She felt uncomfortable and looked away from the girl, unable to meet her mocking and coldly inquiring gaze. Something warned Lily that in the party at the table, Tioga, if that was her name, was not fooled.

Quickly Curly Bill drew out a chair for Lily, allowing her to sit at his right side while the girl, Tioga, sat at the left. He raised a hand which brought up waiters with glasses and a bucket containing champagne.

In less than five minutes Lily had the men eating out of her hand but did not address a word to Tioga, yet she felt the girl's eyes watching her in the same critical manner. The girl lounged back in her seat with the relaxed grace of a cougar on a limb. Her hazel eyes never left Lily's face and the star knew Tioga read her like a book, knew under normal circumstances she would never have spoken to the likes of Curly Bill and wanted to learn what the meeting was leading up to.

'Lord, Miss Lily,' howled one of the men, sitting next to the star and restraining himself just in time from giving her a friendly slap on the shoulder as he and the rest stopped roaring with immoderate mirth at a faintly humorous story she told. 'You're the living wonder.'

Lily's eyes went to the clock behind the bar, estimating how long she had to drive home the iron before Elwin's arrival. The men were eating out of her hand although the girl remained as quizzical as ever. She swung the talk to her show, saw her two assistants standing by the alcove door watching for Elwin, as she ordered, ready to ease him into the bar if he tried to pass.

'The jealousy behind this life makes me think it's not worthwhile,' she said with a heart-rending sigh which made the men feel like they should do something about everything that troubled her. 'It's a terribly hard life for a poor, defenceless woman, Mr. Graham. Alone in a world of petty spite and — and—'

Lily stopped with a sniff and dabbed at her eyes with a tiny silk handkerchief. Curly Bill was instantly the gallant knight in shining armour, ready to come to the fair lady's aid.

'How'd you mean, ma'am?'

'It's nothing, nothing. I suppose I shouldn't mind being kept off the stage for ten minutes while that — that — well, that juggler went overtime with his act.'

'The dirty rat!' growled one of the cowhands.

'Oh, he's young,' replied Lily in the tone of a Christian martyr excusing the lions for eating her. 'But it gets longer and longer every show.'

'Sounds like some kind of a range hawg,' growled Curly Bill. 'Should know a sight better'n treat a sure-enough lady like you mean.'

'He's a tolerable funny *hombre*,' put in Tioga quietly. 'Saw him both times he played in Tombstone. He was good. Thought he might have been a touch better this time but he didn't look to be doing a different act.'

Once more the women's eyes locked. Lily's hate glowed like a living thing although the smile never left her lips. Tioga was startled by the venom in the eyes but not afraid of it. She thought it was as if the painted features of a doll held human eyes behind the smiling mask.

'Of course, my dear,' purred Lily, each word dripping like molasses laced with strychnine. 'We all yield to your good taste. It shows in everything about you. Your hair, your clothes, everything. Not conventional, but bizarre and suiting your personality so well.'

Curly Bill glared a warning at Tioga, not knowing what bizarre meant but guessing it was not complimentary. He expected Tioga to go over the table and land on the star with both fists flying for the girl's temper was likely to be like his own, explosive. Tioga only smiled but it was a smile which

76

made Lily stir uncomfortably in her seat. The girl from the wild country did not know what bizarre meant any more than did Curly Bill. All she knew was that the woman aimed to push them into some trouble.

'Why thank you, ma'am,' said Tioga mildly. 'I always like to hear a much *older* woman's opinions.'

For an instant Tioga thought she had pushed the woman to making more than a verbal attack on her. Lily's fingers curved into claws and her lips lost their smile. In that moment Tioga saw Lily Carlisle as she was, knew for certain that there sat a woman who would move heaven and earth to have her own way. Lily fought down the anger, brought a smile back to her face although it did not reach her eyes and turned to Curly Bill again.

At that moment Elwin entered the bar. He had finished packing his gear away and gone to the woman's room, finding a note on the door asking him to call in the bar before he left the theatre. So he came in hesitating as he saw Lilly seated with the men.

'Elwin darling!' Lily exclaimed, rising 'Come in and meet Mr. Graham.'

The young juggler still hesitated. He did not drink when there was another show later in the day and hardly ever entered the theatre bar. Lily glided over and took his arm to lead him to the table and wave him to a seat. However he stayed on his feet. Suddenly Elwin knew the men were hostile to him and could not think why. During his act they had been among his most enthusiastic supporters, now each man's face held blank dislike.

Curly Bill poured out a drink into the empty glass and held it up, he sat on the opposite side of the table to Elwin.

'Have a drink, juggling man,' he said.

'Not just now, thank you,' Elwin replied a trifle distractedly. He was still worried about Janice, scared of what might have happened while he did his act.

'I don't like that!'

Elwin had been turning away when Curly Bill spoke again, thrusting back his chair and coming to his feet. The dark-faced man's cheeks reddened under the tan and his eyes grew slitted, mean-looking.

Elwin looked back. He knew gunmen; nobody who played the western houses could avoid meeting them at one time or another. Slowly he turned to face the table and the glass which now stood at its edge. He knew what to expect now. His refusal had offended Curly Bill. So the man would make him take drink after drink if he gave in to the first.

'I've got to go—' he began.

'Not until you've drunk with us,' Curly Bill answered.

Now the other men were on their feet also. Tioga shoved back her chair and stood up, her eyes flickering to Lily who was falling back, moving towards the door leading into the theatre. Tioga saw the mocking hate in the woman's face and knew what Lily Carlisle planned. The girl also knew there would be no reasoning with Curly Bill at the moment. Most times she could control him, but right now he was carrying just enough liquor to make him a dangerous-when-wet-proposition. Either the juggler would drink or get badly hurt.

'Perhaps after—' began Elwin.

'Now!'

An awkward and mean old mule could show Curly Bill no pointers in stubborn orneriness when his wild was up. Unfortunately Elwin had some mule in his make-up too and would not back down.

'No!'

There the gauntlet lay, thrown down by Curly Bill, taken up and returned by Elwin. Slowly the dark man pushed back his coat to leave free the matched butts of his Colts.

'I was never a man to take an unfair advantage of anybody, juggler,' he said. 'Sack, put your Colt cocked on the table in front of him.'

The man nearest to Elwin lifted his Colt from leather, cocking the hammer and while it hung at half-cock reached down a finger to move the chamber slightly. Then he lay the revolver on the table in front of Elwin and stepped back a pace.

'It's up to you,' Curly Bill said quietly. 'Take up glass or gun.'

'No, Bill!' gasped Tioga but made no attempt to move.

Suddenly Elwin was scared. He did not want to die. The most important thing in his life was to see that little piece of humanity which for several months now he had been able to feel kicking against him as he lay by his wife. He wanted to live, to teach the boy he hoped for the secrets of a juggler's trade. Yet he did not want to go and see his wife smelling of champagne.

It was then Elwin caught Lily's eyes as she stood at the theatre door. He saw her for the first time as she really was. Read the hate in her eyes, the envy and the jealousy. For the first time the meaning of old Reuben's words began to have a meaning and he knew who Circe was.

'We're waiting, juggler.'

'Hold it, Bill!'

The words came in a gentle, even drawl backed by the click of a Colt coming to full cock. They caused Curly Bill to stand very still and not only the sound of the Colt did this. He knew the voice, knew the man who spoke did not say 'hold it' unless he meant for things to be held.

Looking towards the open street door, Tioga bit down a gasp of relief. She did not know Waco, but could see what he was. Since joining up with Curly Bill, she had learned the signs and could read a man's potential in the gun-throwing line as well as many women followed a dress design. If anybody in Bisbee could make Graham see reason, that man behind the lined Colt Artillery Peacemaker stood best chance of doing it.

The tall young Texan stepped forward, his lined Colt never relaxing. Tioga licked her lips nervously as she saw the danger. Curly Bill would have thrown his lead to wound not kill the juggler, would have had the time to do so. If he matched shots with the Texan that same time would be absent and what started as a hooraw session might wind up a corpse and cartridge affair.

Not one man moved as they watched Waco come nearer to the table. Every man knew who he was, although Tioga did not. They also knew not one of them could move fast enough to down the Ranger before he killed Curly Bill, so they stood fast.

'Howdy Waco,' Curly Bill said, the flush leaving his cheeks as he recognized the newcomer. 'Was just set to teach the juggler it's not mannerly nor neighbourly to refuse a drink.'

'That's a tolerable permanent way to teach a man, Bill,' Waco answered but did not holster his Colt. 'And you're surely taking a chance aren't you?'

Suddenly Waco's left hand dropped, brought up the Colt, lined it on Curly Bill's chest and pressed the trigger. A click came and nothing more. Waco drew back the hammer and lay the Colt down again.

'An even break, huh, Bill?' he asked quietly. 'You could have drawn and put three bullets in Elwin before he cocked back the hammer for a shot with a bullet in the chamber that came under the firing pin.'

Again silence fell on the room. The customers in the bar had been watching everything.

Then Tioga moved. She came forward, throwing back her head and letting out peal after peal of laughter which had some

79

slight touch of hysteria in it. The men stared at her.

'Lord, your faces!' she gasped. 'You too, Bill. All set to have a laugh on the juggler when he grabbed the gun and pulled the trigger. And this gent here turns the game right round on you.' She laughed again. 'Lordy Lord. I ain't had so much funning since my drinking uncle, Silas, picked up a live rattler instead of his rope one morning!'

It gave Curly Bill a chance to back out without gunplay. He did not fear Waco's gunspeed and would have faced the young Ranger if there was need for it. Yet Curly Bill owed Waco something important. He had been captured by an army patrol at a time when the army sought him on a matter of horse-stealing. Through Waco's help he got free and Curly Bill was not a man to forget his debts.

Swinging from the table Curly Bill caught Tioga around the waist and kissed her hard, then held her at arm's length for a moment. He slipped one arm around her shoulder and faced Waco.

'You took a chance with my life there,' he said with a wide grin.

'Likely. Only I couldn't see you being such a fool as let even a man you thought hadn't a chance get that much start. Your pard's like most of us, loads five and leaves the one under the hammer safe. So he slips the chamber back when he takes it out. Only now there's an empty chamber next to the hammer instead of under it.'

'Shucks boy, we was only fixing to throw a scare into the juggler so he'd drink with us.'

'You don't take drink when you've serious work to do later in the day, Bill,' Waco answered. 'So why expect Elwin here to. He's got two more shows today and he can't do them loaded with coffin-varnish.'

'Is there any word from Jan, Waco?' Elwin gasped.

'Wasn't when I came by. You'd best go see,' Waco replied. 'That one drink won't hurt you none, neither.'

Elwin took up the glass, knowing he would not be expected to take more.

'Your lady sickening, friend?' asked Curly Bill worriedly. 'That little blonde gal who sang with you at Tombstone?'

'Not sickening,' Elwin answered, his hand shook slightly. 'No more than any gal having her first baby.'

Instantly all the enmity against Elwin was forgotten. The rustlers of Galeyville were hard and tough men but they, like many of their kind, were sentimentalists. Janice's songs had brought nostalgic tears to their eyes in Tombstone. That she was the juggler's wife raised him in their esteem. That the two were about to have a child set him even higher. In fact some of the party threw hard looks at their boss although usually these six would excuse anything Graham said or did.

'I'm sure sorry about that bit of fooling,' Curly Bill said, coming round the table with his hand held out. 'You wait until you've had the baby, then show or no show we're going to wet its head.'

Lily Carlisle watched all this with blazing eyes. Once more her plans to remove the juggler failed and the same man caused both tries to fail. Her hate left Elwin to come down full on Waco. She fought down the desire to tell her two men to smash Elwin with their fists in some alley. Without killing him the story would get out and not even Lily Carlisle could stand up to the storm of indignation which would rise when people heard. More so as Elwin and his wife were in the process of having their first child.

'That no-good cowhand,' she hissed, turning to walk away. The men moved on either side of her. 'Get him down some side alley and smash him!'

For a long moment as they walked towards the rear of the stage, the two men did not speak to Lily and neither showed the willingness she was used to when ordered to work over some man who incurred her displeasure.

'Did you hear?' she hissed.

'It's no go, Lily,' the taller said. 'We found out who he is. That's Waco, one of Mosehan's Arizona Rangers. If we worked him over this town'd be crawling with his pards so fast we'd not know what hit us. The only way we could stop his mouth would be to kill him and I'm not chancing that.'

'You lousy cowards,' snarled Lily. 'I'm going to the hotel.'

'Want us along?' asked the other man.

'I don't want you any time. Get out of my sight until I have to see you on the stage.'

Lily stormed from the theatre, not even acknowledging the young deputy who held the door open for her. She reached the hotel and was in her room before she remembered she still wore her stage make-up. Screaming at Reuben to arrange a bath for her she cursed more when she heard he had done so. Throwing a vase at him she ordered him to the theatre to fetch her street clothes. Stripping she flung herself into the bathroom, a small room usually used for stowing baggage but now fitted with a bath for her. Splashing water violently she bathed herself and

81

then took her spite on whoever might have to clean the floor by tipping the remaining water over. Lily pulled on her lace panties in the bedroom and slipped her robe on as she heard a knock at the bedroom door.

At the theatre Elwin drank his champagne and departed, followed by Curly Bill's demand that he be let know when the baby came. The dark man took up his hat and looked at the rest of his men.

'Let's go and wind up our business, boys,' he said.

'I'll come with you, Bill,' Tioga suggested.

'Nope, gal,' replied Curly Bill. 'Say, boy, whyn't you take her along to the Grand Hotel for me. We've got us some rooms there.'

An angry glint came to Tioga's eyes. 'I'd rather go with—'

'I said no! Happen you feel like it go out and buy some clothes, or some fancy doo-dads. Tell them I'll pay when I come back.'

With that Curly Bill turned and headed for the door with the others trooping out after him. Tioga stood watching him go, then she turned back to Waco, brought an inviting smile to her lips and waved a hand to the table.

'What say we nibble a few before we start?'

'I don't want none and neither do you,' Waco replied. 'Curly wanted me to see you safe to the hotel and that's what I'll do.'

'And then,' asked Tioga, her voice low and her hands clenched into dangerous little fists.

'Happen you'd like me to take you for a meal I'll do it, someplace that I could eat and not be scared the waiter thought a hawg was at the table. Which same'd be like to happen at the Bisbee Grand.'

'What after that?'

'Take the chip off your shoulder, gal,' said Waco, his voice taking on a harder edge. 'So I'm a lawman, does that mean you reckon Curly Bill could keep me off his back by loaning you to me. If it does I reckon you're selling both me and Bill damned poor.'

Tioga's hand shot out to grip the neck of the bottle. 'I should smash this into your face,' she hissed.

'Happen that's the way you see it, ma'am,' replied Waco quietly. 'You can walk to the hotel without help.'

He reached the door before she caught up to him. 'You're Waco, one of Mosehan's boys aren't you?'

'Sure.'

'Bill talks about you. You saved him one time. Allows that there's only one lawman you can trust, one that totes a Ranger's badge. I got you wrong.'

Waco grinned. 'Why sure. You got a lot of things wrong, gal. First, I've got a law badge but that don't mean I got horns and a forked tail. Bill didn't ask me to take you to keep me from following him. He's known me long enough to figure it'd take a hell of a sight more than the offer of a gal, even one as pretty as you, to stop me taking cards happen I thought he aimed to bust the law hereabouts. Whatever he's doing now, Bill's not looking to breaking the law. I saw him drink and he never does that when he's working. He wouldn't have brought you with him happen he was working either.'

A woman drew aside hurriedly, throwing Tioga a disgusted glance. The girl swung her hips brazenly and leaned closer to Waco until they were past, then drew away again.

'The way she looked at me,' she hissed. 'Like I was some slut from a cat house.'

'Knowed a man one time,' drawled Waco. 'Always said folks looked at him like he was hawg-dirty. He looked in a mirror one day. Know what, he found he'd looked hawg-dirty all the time.'

For a long moment Tioga did not reply. Then she said, 'You're a strange man, Ranger. I never knew one like you.'

'How'd you get mixed in with Bill?'

'How does a gal like me tie in with any man?' she answered. 'I was in a town and Curly Bill rode in. Took a shine to me and when he headed back to Galeyville I went with him. It's something being known as Curly Bill's girl.'

'Huh huh!'

'I know what you think! I'll tell you something, Ranger and you can believe me or not, I don't gave a damn which. But I've never yet bedded with Bill or any man. Nor has Bill ever asked me. We sleep in separate rooms at his place in Galeyville and up at that hotel there's three rooms, a bedroom on either side of the fancy sitting room. I'll be in one room, Bill in the other, both at bedding time and dawn.'

They walked on in silence for a time. The girl glanced sideways at Waco and wondered what he thought about her.

'Whyn't you do what Bill said, go buy a dress, or at best a shirt that's at least a size larger?'

'And let the women in town think they've made me?'

'Thought you didn't like the way they looked at you?'

'How long have you known the juggler?' asked Tioga,

changing the subject to hide her confusion.

'On and off for three years.'

'He's a good friend?'

'Just a man I met and fought alongside in Baptist's Hollow, ran across a couple of times since.'

'Yet you'd have took on Bill and his boys to stop them hoorawing him.'

'That wasn't hoorawing. Bill'd've put lead into him.'

Tioga shook her head. 'Wouldn't have killed him. Might have put a bullet through his arm.'

'Which'd be the same as killing him,' drawled Waco. 'You never heard of, nor saw a one-armed juggler, did you?'

'Man, and I thought I'd seen all the meanness a woman could do,' Tioga said quietly. 'Somebody ought to hand that Lily Carlisle her needings.'

'You forget that, gal,' Waco ordered grimly. 'Lay a hand on her and she'd scream for the law so fast you wouldn't know how come they landed on you. Say, I know a nice li'l place down town apiece. How about coming along and eating with me?'

'Maybe later,' she answered distantly. 'Where're you staying?'

'Down at the Creed. I thought to look in and see how Doc's doing, then I want to send a telegraph message to Cap'n Bert.'

'Then why not come back when you've done it. Bill likely won't be back until morning so I'll be free.'

Waco touched his hat to the girl. He was puzzled by her and wondered what she meant to do. For a moment he thought of trying to get her away from the hotel but before he could speak he saw her turn and walk away.

The desk clerk threw a disapproving glance at Tioga as she collected her room key. Ladies who stayed at the Grand Hotel did not often dress in such a manner. Of course the company the girl was with might account for her taste in clothes. One thing the clerk did not doubt, that man who called himself Graham would not take kindly to anyone insulting his lady friend.

Tioga might have made some remark but she was too thoughtful as she went upstairs. Curly Bill was a rustler, an outlaw, even though nobody had ever got round to proving it in court. He was also generous, genial, kind-hearted within limits. At any other time he would never have thought of calling down a man who couldn't hope to beat him. The woman upstairs brought it about. If Bill had pulled the trigger he would have found himself facing a charge of attempted murder at least. The town marshal of Bisbee might turn a blind eye on Bill's visit as long as he spent money and kept the peace. He would not allow Bill to gun down the juggler and even if Carville, the marshall, did, that tall, young and soft-talking Texan who rode as one of Mosehan's Arizona Rangers would not overlook it. Either way Curly Bill would be in trouble for he was not the sort of man to surrender to the law.

The hall at the top of the stairs was deserted for, apart from Curly Bill's rooms, Lily's was the only suite occupied. On the wall over the side window was a large clock, it showed quarter to five. Soon it would be dark, already the sun was sinking and shadows forming.

Entering her own room Tioga paced up and down in it for a long moment. She came to a halt before the mirror on the wall of the sitting room and looked at herself. She saw in that moment what Waco meant about her dressing like a slut. Tioga's hands clenched and she swore she would buy a decent dress in the morning. Yet there was one thing she could do before she stopped dressing and acting like a slut.

With Tioga to decide meant to act. She hitched up her jeans in a determined manner and left the room, closing the door and leaving the key on the inside. She drew in a deep breath and crossed to knock at Lily's door.

Lily Carlisle wrenched the door open, her enraged curses dying unborn as she saw Tioga instead of either her two musclemen or the dresser stood outside.

'What do you want here?' she snapped.

Tioga put her shoulder down and pushed the door open. Before Lily could close it Tioga stood in the room. Lily fell back a few steps, cold hate glowed in her eyes as she looked at the girl.

'What do you want, shoving in here?' she repeated.

'I just came to see what sort of a woman would set a man up to be killed or hurt bad, just because he got more clapping and laughing on a stage.'

The woman faced the girl; they looked like two cats on a fence. Lily still wore her robe, the front open just enough to show there was nothing underneath it. Tioga studied the woman. Lily stood a couple of inches taller and likely weighed heavier. On the older woman's face lay a look of hate and worse. Suddenly Tioga felt she might have bitten off more than she could chew.

'Get out of here!' Lily's voice rose in a screech.

'When I've told you what I think,' Tioga answered. 'My man

85

nearly ended up trading lead with that young Texas boy. One way or another, happen things went an inch off the trail, there'd have been men die through you.'

'Clear out of here, you lousy little bitch—'

'Old woman. If I'm a lousy bitch and you aren't, I'm surely glad I am.'

Lily's hand swung around, the palm slapping hard against Tioga's cheek, snapping her head to one side and sending her staggering. Then with a scream Lily hurled herself forward, hands like claws reaching. Tioga had been taken by surprise, she hit the wall and before she could recover Lily was on to her. One hand dug deep into Tioga's tawny hair, knotted deep and tearing at it, while the other slashed down, nails aiming at Tioga's cheek.

Pain cleared Tioga's spinning head. Pain and the sudden awareness that unless she acted quickly she would not have much of a face left. Her hair felt as if it was being torn out at the roots but she managed to get her face away from the main force of the claws. She felt a stinging pain as Lily's nails touched her cheek, then they were gone. Lily screamed and lashed her hand across Tioga's face savagely.

Tioga had tangled in hair-yanking brawls with other girls before. She was over the shock now and all set to show Lily Carlisle a thing or two. Her right fist drove into Lily's stomach bringing a croak of pain. It also brought about a relaxing of the grip on her hair. Getting her hands on Lily's shoulders Tioga gave her a push which sent her staggering away.

Only for an instant. Tioga knew she had got herself into something more than she aimed to. She knew for certain when Lily flung herself forward again. They met and tangled like a pair of enraged wildcats, reeling across the room with hands clawing, slapping, punching, pushing, feet kicking and hacking.

Neither made a sound except when pain brought a squeal or cry from their lips.

Tioga hooked her legs around behind Lily and they crashed to the floor to roll and thrash over on it. The buttons of Tioga's blouse popped off and the blouse crawled out of her jeans, leaving bare her round full breasts for the shirt was all she wore. Lily's robe came open, tangling around them, her huge bosom heaving as she fought with the girl.

Over and over they rolled, first one then the other briefly on top. They came to their knees tearing at hair, then threw their arms around each other's neck and smashed down again. Tioga slammed Lily's head against the floor, tossed a leg astride her and sat on her body, knees crushing on either side of the other woman's big breasts.

'Give it up!' gasped Tioga, sobbing for breath.

Lily's back arched and she thrashed wildly but the girl's weight held her. Tioga grabbed down at the woman's hair but before she could do anything Lily had crossed her hands and raked nails down from Tioga's shoulders. The nails bit in hard, Tioga screamed and jerked away. Then Lily brought up her knees, smashing them into the girl's back and throwing her forward off balance. Tioga crashed to the floor and rolled to her hands and knees. Lily also came up and flung herself to the dressing table, dragging open a drawer to reach for an ivory handled paper knife which lay inside. Without knowing what was in the drawer Tioga hurled forward, her arms locked around Lily's waist and they crashed on to the bed.

Over and over the two fighting women thrashed, off the bed and on to the floor to come apart and make their feet. Lily's mouth hung open, the gleam in her eyes was more than anger, it verged almost on madness. Tioga saw it, turned to try and run but Lily was after her and they tangled again, fighting on with the savagery of two primeval creatures.

The door to Lily's room opened. Tioga clung to it, gasping for breath and trying to prevent herself from falling. Her shirt still hung open and had been all but torn from one shoulder, the sleeve having gone. She had lost one moccasin in the fight too. Her left eye was discoloured and swollen, her nose trickled blood which she licked from bruised lips. On her right cheek, across her shoulders and neck were vicious scratches and blood trickled from a bite on her arm. For a moment she leaned on the door jamb, then she stumbled forward, leaving the door open. Pure instinct made her glance at the head of the stairs, but no one was in sight. Her eyes went to the clock on the wall; the time was just gone quarter past five. They must have been fighting for almost half an hour she thought dazedly as she pushed open the door of her own suite.

It took all Tioga's strength and willpower to close and lock the door. The room appeared to be spinning around before her eyes as she staggered across it into her bedroom. Tioga leaned against the bedroom door, closing it behind her. She wanted to get away from the hotel. Her every instinct warned her she must run for she had gone too far this time. Yet the bed looked soft, tempting. It would soothe the ache which filled every inch of her frame. Each scratch and bruise seemed to have developed a separate pain of its own now. She stumbled forward and fell on to the bed. Lying face down Tioga sobbed in pain and the reaction of what she had been through. Then the sobs died away as she seemed to dive into a bottomless pit.

In the office of the town marshal Waco talked with Carville, a big, burly man, well dressed, something of a politician, but a square lawman. He shoved back his hat, rising and held out his hand to Carville.

'I'll tell Cap'n Bert what you said,' Waco promised. 'Reckon I'll be going along to the Creed and see if that baby's made his appearance yet.'

On the wall the clock chimed seven. Carville glanced at it and smiled. The young Texan had held his attention for the past hour. He pushed back his own chair and rose to go for his dinner.

In the Creed Hotel room the coyote wail of a new born baby rang out. Doc Leroy wiped sweat from his face and then dropped his hand to Janice's stomach. He looked at the doctor's wife and she saw the tension in his face.

'Lord,' he gasped, looking at the tiny bundle of life his skill had brought into the world. 'I thought he was a tiny one. Look!'

For the first time in his life Doc Leroy was scared when handling a doctoring chore. The woman wrapped the baby in a blanket and lay it in the cot brought up by the room clerk. Then she turned.

'Go ahead. You've done all right so far.'

The scream of a woman brought Waco on the run to the Grand Hotel instead of visiting his partner. There had formed the usual sort of crowd, people coming from the dining room or passing. They crowded around the reception desk where a woman in a sober black dress was screaming hysterically. Waco saw the young deputy who spent most of his time hanging around the theatre. The young man was racing upstairs with urgent strides which warned Waco there was bad trouble on hand.

Waco forced his way through the crowd, shoving people aside until he was at the front. He looked at the sobbing, hysterical woman and the white-faced clerk behind the desk.

'She's laying on – the bed,' gasped the woman. 'She's dead!'

Waco turned and went for the stairs. The owner of a prosperous mine, pushed aside as Waco went through the crowd, opened his mouth to growl something. He closed the mouth again as he caught the look on Waco's face. In two years as a

Ranger Waco had become fairly well known in Arizona Territory and the mine owner was a man who knew him.

The door of Lily Carlisle's bedroom was open and Waco went to it. The young deputy stood just inside, his face without any colour as he stared across the room.

Lily Carlisle lay face up on the bed, her robe hanging open, her knickers torn. There were bruises on her face and body, one eye was puffed almost shut, the other discoloured and staring dully. Across her naked stomach were four livid scratches torn by clawing nails. From just under the left breast rose the hilt of a knife.

'God!' croaked the deputy as if he was being strangled. 'Look at her!'

His words came too late. Waco had looked and seen all he needed to see. Now his eyes went around the room. The bed was in a state of upheaval, blankets and sheets torn from it and laying on the floor. The solitary chair was broken and lay on its side, the rugs rumpled and scattered, the dressing table swept clear, make-up gear and an empty velvet-lined jewel case scattered as if they'd been thrown at the walls. Among all the tangle and mess lay the sleeve of a shirt and a moccasin.

Scooping up the shirt sleeve the young deputy swung towards Waco, his face twisted in anger.

'That gal with Curly Bill – she had a shirt like this!'

'Sure,' agreed Waco, cursing himself for not having guessed Tioga would come and see Lily Carlisle.

The deputy turned and flung himself from the room, crossing the passage with his shoulder down. He smashed into the door of the Brocious suite and burst it open with almost superhuman strength. The sitting room was empty but a sound in the bedroom sent him across the room. He wrenched open the door and leapt forward.

Tioga, naked to the waist, was trying to force up the stiff sash of the window. She heard a low almost animal snarl, a hand gripped her shoulder and she was dragged backwards. The deputy slammed Tioga into the wall, his hand coming around to snap her head over to one side. She screamed in terror as the hate distorted face loomed above her. The deputy flung wild, hysterical blows at Tioga and the girl's hands came up to protect her face.

'You lousy bitch!' the deputy screamed. 'You lousy, no-good calico-cat, you killed Lily!'

A hand caught the deputy's arm and hauled him away from the terrified girl. He spun around mouthing insane curses and dropping his hand towards the butt of his gun. Then Waco hit him, shooting out a fist with every ounce of strength in his powerful frame. The deputy's head jolted back and he went reeling across the room, losing his balance and crashing down by the wall.

Tioga had returned to the window, weakly trying to force it up. She let out a scream of terror as Waco caught her and thrust her back on to the bed. The scream turned to a terrified and hysterical laugh.

'Quit it, gal,' Waco barked.

By the wall stood a washstand, a jug of cold water at its side. Waco caught this up and threw the water into the girl's face. The hysterical screaming ended and Tioga sat on the edge of the bed gasping for breath as she looked at him.

The sound of voices brought Waco around. The sitting room was full of people, men and women come from downstairs and the floor above. Waco crossed the room and stepped out, closing the door behind him. His eyes ran across the crowd, resting on a plump, matronly woman who seemed to be the calmest of them all.

'Go in there, ma'am,' he said. 'Watch the gal for me. The rest of you get the hell out of here and stay clear of that room across the passage.'

'You can't speak to me like that,' boomed a pompous looking man. 'Who do you think you are?'

'I know who I am, mister. I'm a Territorial Ranger. Now get out of here and send for the town marshal.'

The crowd backed off, all the pompousness leaving the man. Throughout all Arizona Territory one law enforcement body was known and respected. The Rangers acknowledged no man but Mosehan as their boss. When on a case they did not respect persons and civic status meant nothing to them. So the people left the room and stood in the passage outside. Several cast looks at the closed doors of Lily's suite but not one offered to enter the rooms.

Returning to the bedroom Waco looked down at the young deputy. He was now groaning his way to consciousness but would not make any trouble for a spell. So the young Texan turned his attention to Tioga. The girl sat huddled on the bed, her face showing strain and fear as she threw off the sheet the woman tried to drape around her shoulders.

'What happened, Tioga gal?' Waco asked.

'He – he—' she replied, indicating the deputy, 'said she was dead and that I killed her.'

'She's dead. Now get something over you.'

The bite in Waco's voice shook Tioga into some response. She allowed the woman to drape the sheet around her once more. Then she looked at Waco.

'I didn't kill her. Sure we went at it tooth 'n' claw but I didn't kill her. I left her flat on her back on the floor. She was alive. Whining and moaning something awful. But she *was* alive.'

The room door opened and Carville entered. His eyes went first to the girl, then to his deputy and finally to Waco. He bent down and lifted the deputy's head. The young man groaned and tried to get to his feet.

'Her?' growled Carville.

'Me.'

Carville moved clear of the deputy and stood up. 'Why?'

'He went hawg-wild, was like to kill the girl. So I stopped him.'

'Did you have to do it that way?'

'Sure. Which same he's lucky. I don't take to any man mishandling a gal and trying to pull a gun on me when I stop him.'

Ten seconds ticked away as the two men faced each other. Carville could handle a gun but knew he was outclassed by the young Texan. He also knew Waco would not lie.

'Let's take her in,' he said, reaching towards Tioga.

'Why for?'

'She killed Lily Carlisle.'

'You see her do it, marshal?'

Carville glanced at Waco. 'I saw who she came into town with.'

'So what. I rode in with Doc Leroy but I sure enough couldn't handle that baby delivery the way he's doing.'

Waving his hand towards Tioga's bruised face the marshal growled, 'Look at her.'

'You seen Lily Carlisle?'

'Naw, the manager's wife told me when I came in.'

'Get your deputy out of here, then we'll take a look,' suggested Waco.

It said much for the respect Carville held the Rangers in that he obeyed without question. He helped the groaning deputy to his feet, held him as he was about to lunge at the girl and thrust him through the open door. There were two more deputies in the other room and Carville told them to see the young man did not come back inside.

Waco stepped to the bed and looked down at the girl. 'Now

listen to me, gal. Dig another shirt out and put it on. Don't try and run for it again.'

Tioga looked at him with dull, scared eyes. 'They'll hang me—'

'Not unless you did it,' Waco answered, then looked at the woman. 'See if you can tidy her up a mite, ma'am. You going to do what I say, gal?'

'They'll string me—'

'Cut it, gal. Now pass your word that you won't run or I'll hawg-tie you.'

Through all her life Tioga had found little enough cause to trust men in general and lawmen in particular. Yet some instinct told her she could trust Waco and that he would stand between her and any attempt at lynching which might come. He would also do his best to clear her, so she must trust him.

'You got my word,' she said.

Carville looked up as Waco came from the room. The young deputy growled an angry curse but the marshal snapped for him to be quiet. They could hear the rumble of talk beyond the door and exchanged glances. Carville repeated his orders to make sure nobody entered the room and that the youngest was kept out of the bedroom. He went to the door which led to the passage.

The crowd surged forward, faces showing anger, hate, excitement.

'Where is she?' one man asked. 'We can tend to her for you.'

'Get back all of you!' Carville bellowed. 'Nobody's going in that room. There's never been a lynching while I've held the badge and this isn't going to be the first.'

Ugly sounds rolled from the crowd. Waco spoke, his eyes going from man to man in the crowd.

'There's only one way you could lynch that gal. After I'm dead and no man ever killed a Ranger then lived to boast about it.'

The sounds died down. Every member of that crowd knew Carville would halt them by force if need be and backed by the soft-talking Ranger he could hold them back.

'Clear this passage!' Carville roared. 'I'll jail every last one of you for unlawful assembly if you're not gone in five seconds.'

Five seconds later the passage held only Carville and Waco. The two men crossed the passage and entered the death room. Carville let out a low snarl as he looked at the stiff stark shape on the bed. The marshal stepped forward, looking down at the bruised and marked body. Then he turned and walked across the room and picked up the empty jewel case. He moved a scuffed-up rug with his toes and lifted a single diamond earring.

'Her jewel case. And empty.'

Waco nodded, crossing the room to look through the door at one side. 'She was taking a bath, or had been recent which same means she wouldn't likely be wearing any of it.'

'Then the gal took it.'

'Did she?' Waco replied. 'Look around the room. Look at the state both Tioga and Miss Carlisle are in. That gal'd be lucky if she could do more than stand up after a tangle like this. Happen she had knifed the woman, Tioga wouldn't've been able to think clear enough to rob her.'

'I know her kind—'

Waco faced Carville, his voice low and cold. 'What kind?' he growled. 'You don't know anything about that gal, excepting as how she rode in with Curly Bill and she dresses a mite eye-catching.'

'All right. Why'd she go for Miss Carlisle?'

Quickly Waco ran through the incident at the theatre. Carville listened and nodded gravely. 'Never took to her, always thought there was a mean look about her.'

'I should've taken the gal for a meal and talked her out of it,' Waco replied. 'Ought to have guessed what she'd do.'

'Let's go search her room across there.'

'Sure, might be as well to send your deputies to check on the livery barns and stage office to find if anybody's been in looking to get out of town in a hurry!'

'Why?'

'Tioga says she left Lily flat out on the floor. I believe her.'

'Any reason for that?'

Pointing to the scratches across Lily's stomach, Waco replied, 'There was a lot of hate in whoever made them.'

'I've seen gal fights before,' replied Carville. 'Always found them scratched up more or less.'

'Sure. A gal's likely to use her nails. On the face, shoulders, most any place she can get to. Only Miss Carlisle's only got the one lot of scratches.'

With an angry gesture Carville pulled a sheet up and covered the body. 'You seem tolerable eager to prove she didn't do it.'

'I'm eager to get whoever did it. Not take a gal just because she rides with Curly Bill and don't dress the way your wife would. Let's talk with the hotel staff.'

'How come you're getting involved with this?' asked Carville as they walked towards the door. 'It's not a Ranger's usual chore.'

'I was in it from the start. Maybe feel a mite responsible for letting Tioga come up here. I'll set in to the end, happen you don't object.'

'I don't.'

While Carville would not admit it, he did not object to having Waco help him. Carville was a fair man and did not want to take in the girl on a charge of murder unless he could prove she did it. The young Ranger had made a reputation for solving mysterious killings. His help in this case might be important.

Carville brought the hotel staff into the sitting room of the Brocious suite. There were some half a dozen men, women and boys. The severe-looking woman appeared to be over her hysterics now. She sat primly on the edge of a chair while the rest stood. By this time Waco guessed she was the wife of the manager.

'You found the body, ma'am?' Waco asked.

'Who might you be?' she answered.

'This's an Arizona Ranger, Mrs. Mulford,' Carville put in. 'He's working with me on this case.'

'I found the -- Miss Carlisle.'

'What time'd that be, ma'am?'

'Just before seven.'

Waco nodded. He left Tioga shortly before five o'clock. Likely she went right to her room first, then to see Lily Carlisle. If so, the fight would have been over long before seven.

'Why'd you come up here, ma'am?' he asked.

'I hadn't seen Miss Carlisle leave for the theatre and she hadn't sent for any food. I thought I would go along and make sure she was not sleeping. I had the lights on the stairs to attend to so I came up.'

'Had anybody come to see her?' Carville asked.

'How about the two *hombres* in her act and the old timer who acted as her swamper, ma'am?' asked Waco.

'They don't use the front entrance,' sniffed the woman. 'We have a door at the rear for servants.'

'It open all the time?'

The woman sniffed again. 'Of course it is. We can't employ a doorman to take care of the menials.'

'They all come in,' put in the towhaired young bell-hop who had been watching Waco admiringly and clearly was delighted to be able to help. 'The old timer come first, got him a bundle of clothes. He went up there—'

'What time'd that be?' asked Waco.

'Reckon it'd be coming on to six. He was up there about half an hour and come down looking right sprightly I thought. Gave me a nickel and said something about somebody or other not turning no more fellers into hawgs.'

Waco moved forward, towering over the youngster and looking down at him. 'You wouldn't be funning me, boy, would you?'

'Naw. He'd been gone maybe half an hour when the other two came in and went up. They left fast, looked a mite shook up. That'd be maybe ten minutes later.'

'You be sure about the times, boy?'

'Shucks, not to a minute. The old timer came in just afore old Blabb – Mr. Cowley came on to take the reception desk and he starts at six.'

Waco did not reply. He left the room, closed the door behind him and went across the hall to enter the death room once more. There was no pile of clothes in sight. He went through the sitting room and opened the other bedroom door. It contained only trunks and bags, all neatly packed. Waco returned to the Brocious suite and asked the bell-hop if he would recognize the clothes the old man brought. The boy thought for a moment, opened his mouth, closed it again, then shrugged.

'Nope. I wouldn't lie to you, Ranger.'

Carville caught Waco's nod and got the people from the room, thanking them for their help. He closed the door on them and said:

'It doesn't prove the gal didn't kill her.'

'Let's go ask her,' Waco replied.

Tioga sat on the edge of her bed wearing a new red shirt which was every bit as revealing as the other. The dried blood, dirt and tear stains had been washed from her face and her hair was combed into something like order from the tangle it had been. She seemed to have regained some control of herself.

'Feel like telling us about it now, gal?' asked Waco gently.

She nodded and touched her jaw and the matronly woman sitting on the bed beside her moved a little closer.

'I went to see Lily Carlisle and tell her what I thought of her. Reckon I should've knowed better. Anyway we tied into each other. I've took on gals before, but never anything like her. Lord, she scared me. She was like an animal, like she'd gone *loco*. We just fought and fought. Reckon my being younger's all that saved me in the end. I got her flat on the floor, banged her head against it hard. She went limp and I got the hell out of there as soon as I made my feet. Come across and in here—'

'Locking the door behind you—' asked Carville.

'Sure. I was scared loco and knew if she come after me I was done. So I locked the door. I made it in here and fell on the bed. That's all I remembered until I heard them yelling out there. Was just going to change, took my torn shirt off. But I heard that dame scream and knew I'd better get out.'

'Why? You didn't know she was dead,' Carville barked.

'What lawman'd listen to me when Lily Carlisle started caterwauling that I jumped her?'

'So you ran out, gal?' drawled Waco. 'Or tried to.'

'Sure I ran out. I know lawmen. My pappy ran a little cap'n' ball spread back of Tioga City. Weren't much of a place and he weren't that much of a man. He was a dreamer and dreamers don't get far in the West. One night he took a couple of hosses from the Tioga Mine, it was just afore Christmas, he'd been drinking and fixed to give me the first present I ever had. Only he didn't cover his tracks and the next morning the town marshal and two guns from the mine come after them. They wore law badges and didn't even ask my pappy what he'd done or why. They waited until he stepped out and shot him like a dawg, he wasn't even armed. Then one of the deputies got hold of me. I wake up at night smelling his stinking whisky breath on my face. Well I put a knee into him and got free. Did you ever run through the bushes with a man after you. You couldn't have, not for what he came after me for. I was fourteen years old, that's all. I picked up a rock and threw it at him. Saw it hit him. Saw the blood running through his fingers as he staggered away. Then he left me. They burned our house and took every hoss we had, which wasn't many. They just left my p-pappy – I—'

The words ended and Tioga suddenly turned, felt the arms of the woman around her and she started to sob. The woman soothed her like a baby and after a few moments Tioga got hold of herself. She looked towards the two lawmen.

'So now you know why I didn't think to trust any lawman.'

'We're not all like those hired guns up to Tioga,' Waco answered. 'What time about was it when you left her?'

'Almost half past five.'

'And you'd likely get to her around ten to,' drawled Waco. 'You were going at it all that time?'

'Sure. I couldn't get away from her.'

96

'You say you left her flat on her back on the floor?' put in Carville, stepping forward. 'We found her on the bed.'

'I don't know about that. She maybe got up and on to it like I did in here.'

Slowly Waco unbuttoned the cuff of his right shirt sleeve and rolled it up to show the powerful muscles of his lower arm. He stepped forward and held out his arm so the inside faced up towards Tioga.

'I want you to scratch my arm as hard as you can, gal,' he said.

'Why?'

'Just do it, don't ask questions.'

Showing her lack of comprehension Tioga reached out her hand, then started to withdraw it but met Waco's eyes and put the tips of her fingers to his arm. She shuddered and looked at him again but he nodded and she drew down the fingers.

'Harder, gal!' barked Waco, gripping her shoulder with his other hand, the fingers biting in and bringing a gasp of pain. 'Harder. As hard as you can!'

Tioga's fingers bit down into the flesh and dragged along it. Waco's face twisted a little in pain and sweat ran down it. He removed his grip from the girl and her hand came away from him. Waco turned to Carville and showed his arm. Along it were white lines but the skin had barely been broken. He drew down the sleeve, working his fingers.

'Sorry if I hurt you, gal, but it had to be done.'

'What was all that about?' growled Carville.

'Remember those scratches on Lily Carlisle's body?' replied Waco. 'They were deep, angry. Made by somebody with a lot of hate stored up.'

'The gal likely had that same hate.'

'Likely. But she hasn't long enough fingernails to make the scratches and wouldn't only have made the one lot if she had.' replied Waco, pointing to the scratches which showed on Tioga's neck and across her upper chest. Then he took the girl's hand, holding it so Carville could see the short nails. 'I always look at hands when I meet anybody. Remembered that Tioga didn't have any nails at all.'

'I can't stand long nails,' Tioga answered. 'Bill always laughs at me over it. Anyway. I've been tangling with other gals ever since I can remember. I learned early a fist licked scratching in a tangle. I'll use fists, feet, teeth and knees, but I never take time to try scratching.'

There came a knock at the door and the oldest deputy

looked in. 'Got them two *hombres* from the theatre. Had to toss lead into one of them, he went for a gun as soon as he saw us. Found out why. He was toting a fair amount of jewellery a man wouldn't wear.'

'Let's take a look at them.'

'They're out here, Waco,' answered the deputy.

The two musclemen stood in the room, one's shoulder wrapped in a bloody rag. Both looked scared and the taller howled, 'We didn't kill her. She was dead when we got there. All we did was take the jewels for our back-pay and lit out.'

'She was dead when you got there?' asked Waco.

'With that knife she uses for opening letters stuck in her,' replied the man. 'We never done it.'

'I believe you,' drawled Waco. 'You came in, found her dead, saw the jewel box burst open against the wall and helped yourself, then lit out.'

'Yeah,' whined the wounded man. 'We headed for the livery barn to get a hoss each and light out, but the owner kept us fooling around until the deputies come.'

'Likely,' said Carville dryly. 'He's seen enough men wanting to leave town in a hurry to know the signs. So he held you up until my deputies arrived. Take them to the jail. Either of the doctors back in town yet?'

'Nope,' answered the deputy. 'And Waco's partner's still at the hotel with that gal.'

'We never killed her!' howled the taller man.

'Holding you for stealing the jewellery,' Carville replied. 'Take them out.'

The two men were escorted to the door but on opening it found two more waiting outside. The taller man spoke, and was allowed to bring the other in. Waco recognized Reuben, the old dresser and the bartender from the previous night. He brought Reuben forward and eased him into a chair. The deputies took the two men out, closing the door after them.

'Thought I'd best bring him down here,' said the bartender. 'He come in and started to talk about Ulysses and Circe. Then I heard about Miss Carlisle and got to figuring I'd best bring him down here to you.'

Carville scowled at the two men, not understanding what had been said. He looked down at Reuben's left hand as it rested on the old man's knee. His eyes went to the long and dirty fingernails, seeing the rusty red smear on them.

'Just who in hell's this Ulysses you're on about?' he asked.

'Some feller a drunken old pianner player used to tell me

about. Right back in history. Allowed it was Ulysses who finished that gal Circe off in the end.'

Waco moved forward to confront the old man. Reuben's right hand clutched something in his pocket but Waco did not think it was a gun.

'Why'd you kill her?' he asked.

For a moment the old man did not reply. Then slowly he looked at Waco, his face showed recognition.

'I came back from the theatre with the clothes and took them to her room to pack them away. Then I went to see her. She was crawling across the floor and pulled herself on to the bed. She whined and whimpered like a whipped cur dog. The way she had made other people act. Her face – I'll never forget her face. It was old, the face of a vicious scheming hag. I went to help her and she struck me. I fell against the dressing table and looking down saw the knife. I knew then what I must do. What I should have done when she first betrayed me. No longer must Circe be allowed to despoil and ruin the talents of men who fell before her. The knife sank in easily, she writhed twice and then lay still. But that was not enough, I tried to hurt her again.'

'Which same's where the scratches came from,' Waco said quietly to Carville. 'I thought it was him as soon as I saw them. Knew Tioga hadn't the nails to make them. Then when I found the clothes packed away I could have said who did it.'

'Why the hell did he do it?' growled Carville. 'She took him around with her, treated him good.'

The old man came to his feet, drawing back his shoulders and looking towards the others. From his pocket came the left hand with a deck of cards. He laid the deck on the table and squared the edges carefully.

'Now gentlemen,' he said in a far different tone. It had the carrying quality of a man who knew his words must sound all around the theatre. 'Now, as my board of witnesses, I call on you to tell me how many cards you wish me to cut. I would ask you also to assure the audience that none of you know the Great Rube. How many cards, my young friend?'

'Twenty-one,' Waco replied gently.

Squaring the cards the old man make a quick cut and passed the top portion to Waco.

'Count them, sir. Count them aloud. The Great Rube does not wish any deception to be practised.'

Carville opened his mouth to speak but something in Waco's eyes made him close it again. He watched as Waco tossed card after card on to the table, counting as he did so. The last card fell as the young Texan said twenty-one.

'That's right, sir, twenty-one,' Waco said. 'Now if you'd go along with the marshal he'll arrange for your next show.'

Slowly Reuben turned and walked from the room followed by the marshal. Waco stood silent until the bartender spoke to him.

'How did he do it, Ranger?'

'I don't know,' confessed Waco. 'I reckon the Great Rube'll take that trick to his grave.'

Waco lowered the glass of whisky and looked as Elwin rushed up to him in the bar of the theatre. The young Texan leaned on the bar and looked moodily into the glass. A man got nowhere riding a bottle, it didn't even help. He thrust the glass to one side.

'Any word yet?' gasped Elwin.

'We got him,' Waco answered. 'The Great Rube and his Circe both played out their last show.'

'I mean with Janice,' croaked Elwin.

It took a full minute for the words to sink into Waco's mind. There had been little for him to do after the marshal took Reuben away. He went into the other room to talk to Tioga, arranging for her to move into the Creed Hotel as she did not wish to spend another night in the suite. He had watched the awkward shape being taken out of the rear of the hotel and came to the theatre with a desire to get himself stinking drunk. Only after one glass he knew whisky would not buy him anything.

'I'm sorry, Elwin. I just haven't been able to go and see.'

'I went,' gasped the juggler distractedly. 'But Doc chased me away. I've never seen him looking so worried.'

At that moment Doc entered the room. He crossed to the bar and leaned his elbows on it tiredly. He ignored Elwin.

'Four fingers neat,' Doc told the bartender.

Waco watched his partner sink the drink without even giving it time to set in the glass. Sudden panic hit Waco as he watched. Never as long as they had been friends had Doc needed a drink on finishing a doctoring chore. Waco felt tired of death, surely there had been enough dying for one day without this.

'Doc!' screamed Elwin, bringing every eye to him. 'How is she?'

'Which she?'

'Jance of cour – you mean – Doc – you – it's a girl?'

With that Elwin threw back his head and let out a wild howl and turned to start for the door leading into the theatre where another act was trying to carry on through his noise.

'Don't you want to know about your son?'

The words brought Elwin to a halt. He turned to look at Doc who leaned on the bar grinning.

'Son?' gasped Elwin. 'But you said it was a daughter.'

'That too. Mother, son and daughter, all well and healthy, just waiting to see their pappy.'

'Twins!' whooped Elwin, 'Yahoo! I've got twins. We got our own double act!'

The show did not matter any more. The act on the stage gave up and yelled their delight. Show people, stage hands, the orchestra were all up on their feet and yelling in wild delight. The word passed around the audience and suddenly the cheering started.

Waco and Doc stood alone in the bar, even the bartenders and waiters had joined the rush into the theatre.

'Hear you've been working, boy,' Doc remarked.

'You might say that. Doc, you nigh on scared me out of ten years' growth the way you came in here. I was sure something had gone wrong. I never saw you that worried about delivering a baby afore.'

Doc grinned. 'I never delivered twins afore either. Let's go along the street, have a quiet beer and then get some sleep.'

CHAPTER THREE

THE PETITION

THE sage grouse covey blasted into the air ahead of the three horsemen, sailing up and gliding towards the bushes by the side of the trail. They flashed over the trail, no more than wheelruts following the old Indian tracks which in turn used the line taken by the now depleted buffalo herds.

'Sure wish I'd a shotgun,' drawled Waco, watching the birds heading for the rocks and bushes beyond the trail.

Suddenly the leading bird seemed to try and stop his downwards glide, fighting up and away from where he aimed to dip into the bush and out of sight.

'Look out,' yelled Captain Bertram H. Mosehan, pitching sideways from his saddle and grabbing at the butt of his rifle as he fell.

The move came not a moment too soon. A spurt of flame licked from the bush towards which the grouse flew. Mosehan heard the flat slap of a bullet passing over his head, then the crack of a rifle.

Jerking the Winchester from his saddleboot Mosehan lit down rolling, landing at the edge of the trail and diving into the cover of a rock. An instant later Doc Leroy, also holding a rifle, joined him, flattening down at the other side, working the lever and throwing a bullet into the Winchester's breech.

'Where's the boy?' he asked.

Mosehand also realized at the same moment that Waco had not followed them. The three horses were running on at a good speed but all were riderless, nor was Waco hanging Comanche style over the flank of his huge paint stallion. The trail lay empty, Waco's body was not to be seen on it even though the first shot was followed by two more.

At the first sign of trouble Waco reacted as did the other two. First he came off his horse on the side away from the shots, second he grabbed out his rifle. Then he diverged from their movements. He had been on the side nearest to the ambush. He flattened down under a bush and gave thought to his position.

Seconds ticked by as Waco waited for something to happen. His eyes scanned the country around him, the distance first, then the centre ground and finally really close up. Nothing showed, nothing stirred. Only the three shots, each from a different piece of cover.

The men who laid the ambush were not yearling stock at the game. They knew how to handle such a situation and only bad luck broke their ambush up. Such men could be dangerous as a teased-rattler or a starving silvertip grizzly bear. They would not let having their ambush spoiled spook them and would play the game until the last card fell.

Waco remembered Dusty Fog's* often repeated advice on such a situation. 'An army on the defensive is always at the disadvantage.'

Those three men were no army but they stayed on the defensive. They lay up in cover, waiting for a chance to do what they had been paid to do. Waco knew this to be no casual attempt, somebody with a grudge taking a chance on getting the head of the Arizona Rangers. This ambush had been set too carefully, set for one man. Only luck brought Doc and Waco along with their chief, having arrived from a chore earlier that day. Mosehan was in his Tucson office just preparing to ride to Prescott, the Territorial capital to report to the Governor. Waco and Doc claimed they had worked hard enough for a spell and needed a rest, so they would join their boss on his way to Prescott. Now it looked as if they made the right decision. If Mosehan had been alone he would most likely be dead.

Inching his way forward Waco's keen eyes scanned the rough country ahead. He lay at the top of a slope which ended abruptly with a bush in front of an almost sheer wall. Then the range rolled up, thick cover through which a good man might move without being seen unless watched for with care. From where he lay Waco studied the range, working out the positions of the attackers from what he saw in that hectic few seconds of the ambush. One lay under the shadow of a small clump of scrub oaks. The third had been slightly this side of the trees, in a depression of the land. From where he lay Waco could see the hollow and could see just as well there was no man in it.

* Dusty Fog's story is in the author's floating outfit books.

Which same to Waco's mind meant only one thing; The man had decided against passive defence and was now stalking the young Texan. That did not worry Waco. He learned the art of silent hunting from a master and perfected it in still-hunting mule deer and the other easily spooked animals, until he would now bet his life on his skill.

Hefting his rifle Waco started down the slope, moving slowly, every sense alert, keeping to every bit of cover on the way. Somewhere out there the other man also moved. The first to see the other would most surely be the one to walk away from the slope.

'That damned fool boy,' growled Mosehan admiringly. 'Trust him to go over there after them.'

Doc did not reply as he rolled from behind his rock and crawled to a place some twenty yards further on. There he settled down and nodded with satisfaction for he could see the man among the clump of rocks. Not well enough to get a shot, but sufficient to take sight at him.

'Reckon you could draw their fire, Cap'n Bert?' he asked.

Mosehan nodded in reply. He had the other man spotted now and came up to throw a shot towards the scrub oaks. To do so he gave the man in the rocks a target; Up came the man, lining his rifle. Only his head and shoulders showed but he was less than a hundred yards away and Doc's rifle could be relied on to hold true at that range; The heavy rifle bellowed and the man jerked, then flopped forward to hang as limp as a discarded rag doll.

Even as from the other side of the trail came the crash of shots, Mosehan got his chance; The man among the scrub oaks saw Doc and swung up his rifle. The heavy Winchester in Mosehan's hands was already sighted, only needing the trigger touched to send out lead. Mosehan's finger squeezed gently and the Winchester kicked back against his shoulder. He saw splinter kick from the side of the tree and thought he had missed clean. Then the other man came pitching out into sight, landed face down and lay still.

'Waco!' Mosehan roared. 'You all right, boy?'

Through the bushes and cover down the slope Waco moved. The bottom of the wall was hidden by a thick wall of growth, heavy foliage interlaced with thick branches. He thought he had seen a movement on the top of the wall but could not be sure. The other man might have reached it—

There was a trickle of dirt and small stones still running down a part of the wall. Not much; It took keen eyes to spot the trickle and Waco's eyes were keen. That meant, unless he was acting tricky, the man had come down the slope and hidden behind the bushes at the bottom. Either way the man held a momentary advantage if he knew Waco's position.

Easing forward Waco kept alert, for to fail would be fatal. A slight movement caught the corner of his eye. He twisted around, going to one side and not a second too soon. The barrel of a Winchester showed through the bushes, flame lashing from its muzzle. The bullet missed Waco by a scant inch, he felt the wind of it on his cheek. At the same moment he heard the click as the man threw another bullet into the breech. Then Waco's rifle crashed back as he heard shooting from beyond the trail.

The man must have thought his cover would protect him, that the bushes stood a good chance of deflecting the bullet from a .44.40 rifle. In this he made a fatal mistake. The rifle in Waco's hands was undoubtedly a Winchester, had the usual muzzle-long tube magazine under the barrel and the lever action. Yet it did not belong to either the .44.40 centrefire model of 1873 or the .44.28 rimfire model of 1866. The rifle Waco held bore the name Centennial Model of 1876, .45.75 in calibre, throwing out a three hundred and fifty grain bullet by the power of seventy-five grains of powder.

The heavy bullet ripped through bush which might have deflected a lighter load of the more usual model of rifle. Waco saw the other rifle barrel tilt out of line so its bullet sped off harmlessly. He fired again and this time heard for sure the soggy thud of a bullet striking flesh. The rifle in the bushes jerked upwards, there sounded a sudden thrashing behind the bushes and Waco heard Mosehan shout.

'All right, Cap'n Bert,' he yelled back. 'I got this one!'

'And we got the other two. Coming over now!'

'Shuckens, it's a mite late for that,' whooped Waco.

He did not wait to hear if Mosehan made a reply but moved along until he could find a way through the bushes. They did not extend clear up to the wall but left a narrow winding track along the base. Waco's attacker lay sprawled back against the wall, his hands at his side, his head hung over towards his shoulders. For all that Waco kept his rifle ready as he went forward. The precaution proved to be unnecessary. The man lay dead, hit twice, once in the chest, the other in the left shoulder. Waco could have cursed. A man wounded as badly as that would have been easily taken a prisoner. A live prisoner might talk. Then Waco shrugged. This man was a Syndicate gun, one of their better stock from the look of his clothes and the fast man's rig he wore. Such would never surrender without a fight, even when badly wounded. They also would not talk.

Leaning his rifle against the wall Waco bent over the man. He appeared to have been in his late thirties; his face was not familiar to Waco and likely did not appear on any recent wanted poster if it ever had. The Syndicate did not use wanted men for hired killers unless they were pushed hard.

Quickly Waco went through the man's pockets but apart from some fifty dollars in gold and small bills, a sack of Bull Durham tobacco and a few matches there was nothing. No letters, not a thing to identify the man as had been the case when other Syndicate men died on a kill.

Waco took up his rifle, forced his way through the bushes and heard Doc call, 'This'n's cashed.'

The young Texan climbed the wall and made his way to where Mosehan stood in the scrub oak clump looking down at the third killer.

Waco joined his boss, his eyes going to a raw gouge ripped in the side of the tree, then down at the man. The heavy flat-nosed bullet had torn through the wood on the glance, coming out low in a ricochet which caught the man under his collar-bone and, spinning like a buzz-saw, ripped down into his chest cavity.

'Lord, these new Winchesters are real mean guns,' Waco said quietly.

'He's Kinsey,' Mosehan answered. 'Knew him from back when I first ran the Hashknife outfit. He wasn't quite dead when I got to him. He said something about telling somebody called Jack Faye that I'd the devil's own luck.'

Doc came up, rifle under his arm, from checking the man he shot. 'Dead. Hit him between the eyes. Never saw him before, or can't remember him at all. Good stock hired killer from his clothes and gun. Nothing in his pockets.'

'Kinsey's one of the Syndicate's top guns, isn't he?' asked Waco, his earlier thoughts getting confirmed by the second.

'About the top, since Dusty Fog cut down Iowa Parsons in Tombstone three years back,'* agreed Mosehan.

'It don't look like they cotton on to us taking so much notice of them the last few weeks,' said Doc.

For the past two months the Rangers had mounted a growing offensive against the Syndicate, the unknown organization who ran the crooked gambling houses, saloons, dancehalls and

* Told in GUN WIZARD.

106

brothels in almost every town in Arizona Territory. In their investigations the Rangers had managed to padlock several places, even in the face of some political opposition and some complaints from local lawmen. Yet the Rangers had gone no further forward than any other group who tried to get behind the face of the Syndicate. Who the men behind it, the powers who ruled the great octopus-like group, might be Mosehan did not know. So thorough was the organization of the Syndicate, so great the fear they held their people under, that none knew, or would dare tell even if they knew, who ran the town for the Syndicate.

In the early days of the Rangers Mosehan tried to ignore the existence of the Syndicate for there was much crime to take the attention of his thirteen-man force. However it always nagged at his conscience, always was the thought that he had turned a blind eye to the most powerful criminal force of all. Then a good friend, owner of a straight saloon received notice the Syndicate wanted in on his place. His boys smashed one attempt at wrecking the bar then a few days later he stepped from his house to walk to the saloon and a rifle bullet cut him down.

That proved to be the spur Mosehan needed. He brooded and blamed himself for the killing, thinking if he had moved earlier Ed Bulek might still be alive. With that thought Mosehan give his orders. Smash the Syndicate. His men needed no further instructions. They moved fast, struck hard. This ambush showed the Syndicate had felt the sting of the lash and were striking back.

The Syndicate lived by fear, existed only because no man so far dared cross them. Three years before, a Syndicate man tried to run an operation outside their usual line, working alone. He failed in it due to the gun skill of Waco's old friend and hero, Dusty Fog. It took the Syndicate almost six months, several brutal beatings and a killing to restore their former hold over the unwilling subjects of their evil empire. Now they wouuld not dare let anybody, even the powerful Arizona Rangers, go against them without striking back.

'You said something about this *hombre* mentioning a name.' Doc remarked.

'That's right,' agreed Mosehan. 'Faye, Jack Faye. It might have been one of the other two.'

'Likely,' Dock drawled.

'How much do you know about the Syndicate, Cap'n Bert?' Waco asked.

'Not much. Just little things I've been gathering ever since I took over the Rangers. One thing I've learned is that all the ordering of guns is done by a single man. Who he is and what he is I don't know. All the Syndicate's guns get their orders from him but only the best ever get to meet him.'

'There's a Faye rides with Curly Bill's bunch over to Galeyville,' Doc remarked. 'I don't know what his first name is.'

'Tom,' answered Mosehan, 'and it's rode with, not rides. Tried to show the others how tough he was by taking a herd of Texas John Slaughter's cattle. Don't reckon he was as tough as he made out. They found him propped against the door of Babcock's saloon one morning. A bullet hole between his eyes and no sign to show how he came to be there.'

'That's Slaughter's way,' said Waco grimly.

'Yeah,' agreed Mosehan. 'That's Slaughter's way. But it lets out that Faye!'

'Nothing in their pockets, never is when the Syndicate sends them on a kill,' Doc remarked. 'What'll we do with them.'

'Could take them on to Prescott,' Mosehan replied.

'Mighty try backtracking their hosses,' Waco suggested. 'Leave the bodies here and send a wagon for them.'

'Try it,' Mosehan ordered, knowing Waco's skill at following a track.

In this case the tracking skill served little purpose. The three killers had left their horses well back from the trail. However their tracks proved they came from the Prescott trail only a short distance above where they set up the ambush. On the hard surface of the trail not even Waco could say which way the men came although he guessed at Prescott.

So Mosehan gave the order to his two young Rangers to ride on towards Prescott. There they would ask Ned Draper, the town marshal and a honest lawman, to collect the bodies whilst they began their search for a man called Faye, a man who might for all they knew be laying dead out there, killed in the ambush which failed.

For the period Prescott could call itself a large town. As Territorial Capital of a prosperous territory it had grown well. Around the edges it might resemble any other frontier town with its general stores, saloons, dancehalls, and gambling houses but towards the centre, where stood the Governor's mansion and the seat of the territory's government, it resembled, in layout if not in building materials, an eastern

108

township. The central area had its own shopping centre, not the general store which was likely to stock everything and anything a man could use, but small separate establishments dealing in only a few commodities. Downtown the cowhands or mineworkers might behave as in any other such area throughout the territory but by tradition if they came up this way they stayed sober and behaved politely.

The sun was setting and few people walked the streets of the town centre as Mosehan, Waco and Doc rode along. The three men attracted no attention, or very little for while Doc and Waco only visited Prescott rarely Mosehan was well known as head of the Arizona Rangers.

The sights of the town centre interested Waco. He studied them, grinning with delight at the rare and unusual idea of having two buildings, one selling men's clothing, the other women's. In most towns man and women shared the same building, any fitting being done in the storekeeper's back room.

'Just look at those hats,' he said, pointing to the lighted window of a small shop. 'Man, I'd sure like to see Big Em from Fort—'

The words died away as Waco saw the name painted on the glass panelled door. 'JAQFAYE of PARIS.'

'What's wrong, boy?' demanded Mosehan.

No casual observer would have noticed the change in Waco's attitude, Mosehan and Doc saw the slight stiffening in Waco's appearance and detected a message in it.

'Now how'd a man read that name?' Waco replied.

The other two directed their glances towards the door as they slowly rode on by. Mosehan gave a low grunt of disbelief.

'Not him, boy. I've never seen him, but the Governor's wife and near on all the big ranch owners' and miners' wives buy their hats and clothes from him.'

'It'd read tolerable like Jack Faye though,' Waco drawled.

The shop had a small window on either side of the door and through them the men could see inside. From all they saw the owner did not appear to be in the front and Waco brought his horse towards the sidewalk.

The three men dismounted on the sidewalk and stood looking through the window once more. Inside the building was a small counter, several comfortable chairs, hats and dresses on wire dummies. To one side of the counter a door led apparently to the owner's living quarters or office, for it had

109

'Private' painted on it. A full-length mirror set into a wall along from the door, several curtain-doored fitting rooms lined the far wall. The counter had a couple of hats and a mirror in a swivel mounting on it, beyond that nothing indicated this shop to be a place of business.

'I'll go in first,' Waco said. 'He'll likely know you even if he's not the one. This way there'll only be me make a fool of myself.'

'Why try, boy,' grinned Mosehan. 'You've done it before.'

For all that Mosehan stood at the right of the door so as to be out of sight from inside while Doc took his place at the left. Waco opened the door and stepped inside. He crossed to the counter, looking around. A bell tinkled as he opened the door but so far the owner did not make his appearance. The young Texan looked around him with interest, grinning at some of the more intimate forms of female garment tactfully displayed in a curtained alcove at the side of the room away from the fitting cubicles.

'May I help you?'

A middle-sized, slim and rather foppish-looking man stepped from the door marked 'Private'. Everything about him looked foreign to Waco's eyes. His face had a pencil thin moustache and tiny beard, his eyes were dark. In dress he wore the height of eastern fashion, wore it fussily like a man who took more than ordinary care of his appearance. He moved with a cat-like grace, almost mincing yet with a lithe spring to his step which did not escape Waco's eyes. To the young Texan it spelled danger. This effeminate-looking man carried himself with the grace of a swordsman, a master of the singing blades.

'You Jaqfaye?'

'I am Pierre Jaqfaye, *monsieur*. May I help you?'

Waco leaned on the counter. He had not shaved that morning and crawling in the bush did not leave his clothes in the cleanest or best of shape. All in all he looked just how he wanted to look. Like a mean two gun hardcase on the lookout for work.

'Kinsey told me to look in on you. Allowed you might need a man with a fast gun.'

Not by as much as a flicker of his eye did Jaqfaye show any sign of expression at the words. His face looked too expressionless altogether.

'Kinsey? I am afraid there is some mistake. You have the right person?'

'That's what Kinsey told me. I met him out a piece, right

after he'd cut down Mosehan. He told me to come along here and ask you if you were hiring.'

Once more the face had too little expression for an innocent man. The slim shopkeeper's eyes took in every detail of Waco's appearance, and his lisping voice went on:

'This is all beyond me. I know nothing of which you talk. Also I am a very busy man with no time for fooling.'

A hard grin came to Waco's lips. 'So play cagey. But stop fussing me, mister. I've no time to waste here either. Kinsey said he'd come with me but he was heading for the hideout.'

'I see. Wait a moment.'

The man turned and stepped back into the other room. Waco leaned on the counter and watched the door. Then the corner of his eye caught a movement reflected in the mirror on the counter. Without making it obvious he looked in that direction. The big mirror set in the wall appeared different somehow. Then Waco got it. The mirror had moved slightly, not much but enough for a man to be able to peer out through the crack by the side of it. He knew what must be happening. In the back room a man studied him.

The mirror drew in again and Waco called, 'Hey *hombre*, happen I'd best go tell the local law about Mosehan.'

The office door came open rather hurriedly and Jaqfaye returning, a shining black walking cane in his hands. He studied Waco once more and asked, 'You still wish to work for us?'

'Why sure, happen the money's as good as Kinsey said.'

'Then come with me.'

Jaqfaye started to walk towards the door, Waco moved from the counter and the man turned towards him.

'Ah! I have left my gloves on the shelf under the counter. Would you lean over and collect them for me, *monsieur*, please, I never like to walk out without them.'

'Why sure,' agreed Waco, turning.

The young Texan felt the hair on the back of his neck rise stiff and bristly as he reached over the counter. Jaqfaye stood behind him, feet apart, right hand gripping the top of his walking cane, the left holding it across his body, twisting slightly at the wood. Something didn't quite fit in the way the Frenchman acted.

A low click came to Waco's ears, then a soft footfall. Pure instinct sent Waco to one side. He heard the hiss of steel and something struck the thin wood of the counter front, sinking through it. Waco heard Jaqfaye's startled exclamation and felt the man stumbling against him. His elbow drove back as

111

hard as he could propel it, smashing into the man's stomach. Jaqfaye let out a croak of agony and stumbled backwards but Waco did not get a chance to act against him.

The door at the rear crashed open and a man flung himself out, a gun in his hand. Waco's right had dipped, flame spurting from the barrel even as the man threw down on him. The bullet fired by the man missed Waco, his own shot struck up under the man's jaw, throwing him backwards, the top of his head shattered open where the .45 lead charge came out. Regretfully Waco shot to kill, shot at the only place he could be sure of an instant kill. The gunman's lifeless body spun around, hit the wall then went down.

Already Jaqfaye had recovered. His left hand lashed under his coat and a Remington Double Derringer slid clear of it. Even as he was about to shoot, he heard a crash and the door behind him burst open. Doc Leroy came through it fast, his right hand seemed to make no more than a slight-defying flicker but ended with the ivory-handled Colt rocking against his palm. Like Waco he shot to kill. With the Derringer lined on Waco's back, hammer drawn ready to fire Doc could not even think of shouting a warning. Jaqfaye pitched to one side, his body smashing on to the floor.

Mosehan entered the shop, closing the door behind him. Waco stood by the man he killed, looking down. Then he nodded and turned to Mosehan.

'He knew me. Must have been in there with Jaqfaye. Then when Jaqfaye heard me out here looked and recognised me. I thought there was something in the way Jaqfaye didn't holler for the law. He's the man we wanted.'

'Check the back room,' Mosehan answered. 'I'll hold the folks outside as long as I can.'

So while the two Texans stepped into the back room of the shop Mosehan went outside. Already people were gathering on the street, a few even almost at the shop, but they slowed to a halt when they saw the head of the Arizona Rangers.

'What happened, Captain Mosehan?' asked a portly businessman. 'We heard shooting in Jaqfaye's.'

'Hold up,' lied Mosehan, not wishing the full facts known until his men had time to search the shop. 'My boys saw the man inside. But they were too late to save the owner. He's dead.'

By now the town marshal and two of his deputies came into sight and Mosehan prepared to carry out his deception with official co-operation.

In the back room of the shop Waco pointed to the safe, the door was closed but the key was still in the lock. Evidently Jaqfaye had been interviewing the gunman when Waco made his appearance and came out to talk with the young man.

'Shouldn't look in there by rights,' Doc drawled as Waco pulled open the door of the safe.

'We're not likely to miss the chance, now are we?'

Saying this Waco opened the door of the safe and looked in. On the top shelf lay a roll of stiff paper which looked familiar. Waco took this out and a small notebook he found underneath it. Doc however looked at the open cash box on the second shelf. This he opened and gave a low whistle.

'I never thought there'd be this much money in selling women's clothes.'

Waco glanced down at the box, then lifted a sheaf of the money out, he ran it between his fingers like a professional gambler riffling a deck to check if they were marked. He replaced the money and took a second pad.

'They're all ones, fives and tens,' he said. 'Which same's tolerable strange in a place like this. I saw some of the prices on his gear. Women who brought them'd be like to pay by bank draft, or with fifty dollar bills.'

'So?' asked Doc.

'So a hired gun who started showing fifties and twenties'd be like to attract some attention. Pay him in small money and he'll pass it with no trouble.'

'Could be. How do they get hold of Jaqfaye to ask for the gunmen?'

Waco grinned at Doc. 'There you've got me.'

Waco heard voices in the other room and unrolled the paper from the top shelf. It proved to be an ordinary army map of Arizona Territory with every town named – and numbered. Waco looked the map over, the numbering had been done after it came from the army for the numbers were written in pencil.

'What's in the book?' asked Doc.

Opening the small book Waco found a list of numbers at the side of each, neatly printed, a name. In the book were a couple of telegraph message forms which Waco took out and read. The first ran:

'Send two size 9 dresses, Ogden.'

The second, 'Send three size 4 dresses, Handley.'

Turning a page in the book Waco found it to be an account

of something or other. In the first column was written a date; in the second a number, mostly under five; in the third another number, going up to thirty, then finally a name.

'Put the rest in the safe,' Waco said. 'I'll take the map and book.'

Doc did not argue with his young friend. He pushed the cash box back into the safe and closed the door. To Doc's surprise, Waco then locked the safe, removed the key and slipped it into his pants pocket. Then Waco folded the map flat and put it and the small book inside his shirt front.

'Let's go and meet the boss,' Waco suggested.

'I surely hope you know what you're doing, boy,' replied Doc.

'Ever know me when I didn't?'

'I never knew you when you *did*.'

A small group of people waited in the shop with Mosehan and the town marshal. All turned as the two young Texas men stepped out of the back room and came towards them. A portly well-dressed man, a minor politician, Waco guessed, stepped forward.

'Well?' he demanded pompously.

Waco looked through the man. No member of the Arizona Rangers answered questions unless asked by someone with authority over them. Throughout the whole of Arizona Territory that meant only two men. Captain Bertram H. Mosehan and the Territorial Governor himself – and this portly, pompous man was neither.

'Did you get them?' the portly man went on.

'Nothing out back, *Cap'n*?' drawled Waco, placing great emphasis on the last word. 'We looked real good.'

The portly man waddled across the room and peered into the office at the rear. To Waco's eyes the man showed some relief when he came out once more. Mosehan watched Waco, a cold gleam in his eyes. It took a good poker player to read that expressionless face and Mosehan was not only a good player, he was an acknowledged expert. Waco was hiding something but Mosehan knew better than ask about it.

By now the town marshal had organized the removal of the bodies and he cleared the shop of onlookers. Mosehan followed him and turned the key in the lock after the last left.

'What's that all about, Bert?'

'The boy's got something to tell us, Ned,' Mosehan answered.

114

Throughout the Arizona Territory there might be found a scattering of lawmen who did not like the Rangers but Ned Draper of Prescott was not one of them. He and the Governor between them selected Mosehan to run the Rangers and Draper knew the Ranger Captain never made wild statements.

'Let's take a look in the back room first, shall we?' Waco asked, indicating the window through which a morbid group of spectators looked.

'Now what's this all about?' Draper asked, entering the office.

'You been housing the boss of the Syndicate guns, that's all,' replied Waco.

'He the one, boy?' Mosehan inquired.

'The big augur his-self,' agreed Waco.

'Need proof of it.'

'Way he acted out there's fair proof, Cap'n,' drawled Doc.

Draper's eyes jumped from one to another of the Rangers like a cat on a hot stove lid. Finally he could restrain his curiosity no longer.

'What the hell's all this about?' he asked. 'I come here, find Jaqfaye and a man stretched out cold, both holding guns. Then see Jaqfaye's swordstick stuck out of the counter. Now you talking about the Syndicate. It all tie in?'

'Ties in with three men who tried to kill Cap'n Bert out of town a piece. The late Mr. Kinsey being one of them. Him and two more laid for Cap'n Bert and died through it. Only afore he died he said what we took to be Jack Faye, two words. Then on the way in to tell you we saw the sign outside. Cap'n Bert and Doc stayed out there and I come in, let on I was a gunny looking for work and had been sent by Kinsey. First off that *hombre* didn't bite. Then I reckon he thought he'd get rid of me. Only he didn't start to holler for the law like he would had he been what he made out to be. Come in here. The gunny was here, likely looking for orders.'

Stopping speaking, Waco crossed the room to a side door, opened it and looked inside. The room led to the rear of the building and in it was a bed, table and chair, the bed not having been made since morning. A panel at one side of the room caught Waco's eye. Crossing to it he gave a gentle push and it slid open an inch or so.

'Look through here, marshal,' Waco drawled.

Stepping to Waco's side, Draper looked through the crack into the shop itself. 'Be behind that big mirror,' he guessed.

'Sure. The gunny was in here, likely this's where their men hide out if they don't want to be seen around town,' agreed Waco. 'He knew me, must have told Jaqfaye who I am. Jaqfaye come out and said he'd take me to one of the bosses. Only he aimed to kill me. I'd seen a swordstick afore and guessed what he planned. Then after I handled Jaqfaye the gunny jumped me and I had to kill him.'

'Who got Jaqfaye?' Draper asked.

'Me,' drawled Doc. 'He was lining on the boy's back and needed stopping fast.'

'We came in here,' Waco continued. 'Checked through the safe.'

Draper stepped to the safe door and tried it. 'Locked,' he said.

'Sure,' agreed Waco. 'It's locked *now*. I locked it.'

'Why?'

'Like this, marshal. There's some powerful, real influential folks in the running of the Syndicate. Likely some of them'd like to make sure there's nothing in that safe to point the finger at them, or show what Jaqfaye did beside selling women's clothes. So I locked the safe and left it like we'd not managed to get in. It gave me a chance to talk to Cap'n Bert and you about what it'd best to do.'

Mosehan and the others watched Waco, knowing full well he had planned every move. The marshal glanced towards Mosehan and received an encouraging nod in return. More than the head of the Rangers, a town marshal, especially the town marshal of Prescott need be something of a politician. If the young Texan called his play wrong the resulting political storm would cause heads to roll and Marshal Draper's would be among the first.

For all that Draper's faith in the ability of the Rangers made him decide to play along with them. He hated the Syndicate and all it stood for, hated it as only an honest lawman could hate a corrupting and evil force. If the Syndicate could be smashed Draper wanted to help smash it and from the looks of things there might be a chance to break it here. Never had anyone got so close to the top of the Syndicate as right now. Jaqfaye, the man who hired their guns and sent them on their deadly errands, must be high among the rulers of the Syndicate. In the past lesser members of the organization fell to the law but they either did not know the men above them or, by fear of what might happen to them or their kin, dare not talk.

'We'd best talk this out,' Mosehan said. 'It'd look tolerable suspicious if we stayed here to do it.'

'Could go down to the office,' Draper suggested.

Waco saw the snag in this. 'How about this key?' he asked. 'I've got something out of the safe and I'd like to put it back if you reckon that'd be the best way to play it.'

'Easy enough. Down to the undertaker's they'll prepare the corpses for burial and when they do I always get all the effects to be held until their kin or somebody with authority takes it. I make inventory of what's brought so we can always get the keys in then.'

This arrangement proved satisfactory to Waco and so they returned to the front of the shop. Draper called in two of his deputies and told them to see to getting the bodies to the undertaker's. Then he left with the Rangers and they mounted their horses to ride alongside him on his way to the office.

Standing near the capital building, the marshal's office looked little different from a thousand others in a thousand towns. The size changed, the building material varied from adobe bricks to mud or stone, the faces might differ but the general layout never really altered. There was always the same desk, mostly scarred by spurred heels and burning cigarette tips; the same sort of weapons, the Winchesters and double-barrelled ten-gauge scatterguns on the wall; the inevitable wanted posters on the walls, the doors leading to the cells, the marshal's office and the deputies' room. Prescott's office differed little except that, as fitting the office of the Territory capital, the desk remained unscarred.

Escorting the three Rangers into his private office Draper paused at the door to tell the desk man he did not wish to be disturbed. Then he closed the door and crossed to take a chair at the desk waving the others into seats and reaching for the office box of cigars.

'Not for me, thank you 'most to death,' drawled Waco, taking out his makings and hand-rolling a smoke. 'Man, you sure live well. Only time there's any smoking in Cap'n Bert's office's when we get the makings out.'

Draper grinned, then became serious. 'Just what's this all about?'

'Like we said, we hit one of the top men of the Syndicate,' Waco drawled.

'Jaqfaye?' Draper grunted, still not able to believe what he'd been told and looking for stronger confirmation. 'A dressmaker. He acted more like a woman than a man most of the time.'

'Knowed a woman 'bout three years back,' drawled Waco. 'Name of Considine.* She was as tough and a damn sight meaner than any man I ever met.'

'Meaning?'

'That Jaqfaye now, marshal. Tell you, he near shoved that sword of his cane clear through me. Handled it as slick as I've ever seen one used. He moved real fast and mean. So he sold women clothes, so maybe he didn't go around drinking and busting up bars. You reckon he ought to have hung out a sign telling folks he hired guns for the Syndicate?'

'You made your point, boy,' said Draper. 'I just wanted reassuring.'

'I knowed that from the start,' grinned Waco. 'Anyway he was perfect for the part. I tell you I near on thought we'd picked the wrong man when I first saw him and only went through with it on chance. When he didn't start hollering for the law I knew we'd struck pay dirt.'

'How's he get to know where and how many guns to send?' asked Mosehan. 'If we can get the contact men we might find the Syndicate's bosses. Could even bust them down like quail in the north forty.'

'Never saw you hit a quail, Cap'n Bert,' drawled Waco. 'And likewise I know how he got to know. The man who delivers the messages'd be right easy to find. He handles the telegraph key at the post office.'

Draper came to his feet angrily. 'I've known Rufe Checker down at the post office for years. He's not in the Syndicate.'

Waco looked up, meeting the angry eyes without flinching. 'Pull in your horns, marshal. I only said he delivered them. He doesn't know but they're any different from a dozen others of the same kind he takes to Jaqfaye's shop.'

With that Waco pulled the map from his shirt and spread it out for the other men to see. Then he opened the little notebook and tapped it with his forefinger.

'There's some numbers in this book, same as on the map and by each number some writing most likely in French. I figure this tells who the contact man in each town is.'

'Why?' asked Mosehan.

'Easy enough. Prescott doesn't have a number, nor does any small place that likely hasn't a telegraph office.

The other men examined the map, seeing what Waco said

* Told in RETURN TO BACKSIGHT.

to be true. Draper took out the telegraph forms from the note-book and looked at them then shook his head.

'Look like an ordinary couple of orders,' he said.

'Way I read it somebody in Tombstone needed some help,' Waco replied, indicating the top form. 'Going by the numbers on the map and the dress size. Look, send two size nine dresses. I read it that the man wants two gunmen and number nine on the map's Tombstone.'

'Could be the other way around,' Doc remarked.

'Nine guns, that'd be a tolerable amount of trouble. So much that we'd have heard about it by now,' Waco answered. 'But the nine in the book's something I don't understand.'

Draper stretched out a hand, taking his seat once more. He turned the book around, studying the list for a moment, then sat back with an air of concentration.

'It's *Cheval D'Or* and *Boucher*,' he finally said. 'I was born in New Orleans and learned to speak French almost better than English, only it's been some years since last I used it.'

The others sat back smoking and waiting while Draper fought back through the layers of his memory to regain the knowledge of French he had once commanded. He rose and paced the room, lips moving to unspoken words. At last he sat at the desk and took the notebook up again.

'*Cheval D'Or* means horse of gold and *Boucher* is butcher,' Draper said. 'If it helps any.'

'Horse of gold!' mused Mosehan aloud. 'There's a Golden Horse saloon in Tombstone, but I don't get the butcher part.'

'Frank Ogden runs it,' Waco put in and for once his excitement showed. 'He's got a barkeep they call Butch. I often wondered about Butch. He never does his fair share of the work and Ogden didn't strike me as being the sort of man who'd let a hired hand get away with it unless he had to.'

'Frank Ogden's a honest man,' Mosehan put in.

'Which same never worried the Syndicate yet,' drawled Doc. 'They've took over more than one honest saloon in their time.'

'There's something a mite stronger than just guessing here,' Waco went on. 'This Butch wants help and goes to send a wire. Now he's not likely to be the sort of man who can afford to buy his wife clothes from Jaqfaye, even if he's married. So he sends the messages as if Ogden told him to. That way the man on the telegraph key in Tombstone doesn't get suspicious as Ogden can afford to buy clothes from Jaqfaye.'

Draper was scanning the list eagerly, taking a sheet of paper and pencil to copy the numbers then translate the names. 'This way we've got the main contact man in each town.'

'Likely the only contact man,' Waco remarked. 'The Syndicate wouldn't want too many folks knowing who their boss gun was.'

'We know them in every town but one,' Doc put in.

'Which one?'

Doc grinned at Mosehan who asked the question, 'Prescott.'

'Likely never needed one, with having Jaqfaye here,' drawled Waco. 'Who'll get Jaqfaye's belongings? Is he married?'

'Got nobody that I knows of,' replied Draper. 'It'll be in the hands of his attorney, if he has one.'

'I'd guess he will have,' said Waco, looking at the book. 'The Syndicate know something might happen to him. They know about this book he keeps. So they'll have it fixed that if anything happens to Jaqfaye one of their other top men can get the books.'

'Which means the man who claims the belongings will most likely be the one we want,' Draper put in.

'Likely,' agreed Waco.

Mosehan looked at the book and grunted. 'Jaqfaye keeps books, that means all the others keep them. Make sure they don't dip their hands into the Syndicate pot. That means the head man keeps a set of master books that'd blow them wide open. If they fell into the wrong hands.'

Waco grinned. 'All we've got to do is find the right set of books and the man who owns them then.'

While this went on Draper wrote the names, translating them from the Fench and making a list of the contact men for the Syndicate in each town. Some of the names brought a whistle of surprise from Mosehan. There were pillars of society and ordinary workmen among the names, none of them apparently connected in any way with the others. The Syndicate's net took in all kinds and these men on the list were the local heads, the top men in each town. They must be the leaders for they all knew the secret of Jaqfaye's dress shop and none but the heads of the towns and the most trusted of the guns contacted him.

'What're we going to do now?' Waco asked when the list lay before them.

'Could put the notebook and map back, but it'll likely disappear and never show again,' Mosehan answered. 'I'd like to keep it in evidence, just in case we ever get the other books.'

'Why not?' Draper asked. 'The safe's locked. We put the safe keys in Jaqfaye's pocket and the Syndicate don't know what to think. They won't know for sure if we opened the safe and are playing smart, or if their own man's trying to double-cross them. I've never known crooks who trusted each other, not that kind of crook anyway. One way and another there's going to be some stirring up done.'

'That's it,' agreed Mosehan. 'I reckon with what I know now I can get Frank Ogden and some of the other honest saloon owners to dig their heels in. Then the contact men'll try to get hold of Jaqfaye for help. It'll take the Syndicate some time to organize another safe way of getting their guns out and by that time more folk'll've started to fight back.'

'It'll be risky for the men who start digging,' Draper warned.

'Sure, but I'll have them covered by my boys. We'll just have enough start so that I can cover them, say four or five of them. That'll be all we need. Once a thing like this starts moving and one gets away with it two more make their play. We can split the Syndicate apart at the seams if we play right, fast and lucky.'

'How about us, Cap'n Bert?' asked Doc. 'Who do we cover?'

'You? Why didn't you know? There's been a threat to shoot the Governor and you're staying on in Prescott to help guard him. You also have to keep watch on whoever takes possession of Jaqfaye's effects. Then watch him until he contacts the rest of the Syndicate. This's our chance. We'll play this out and when we get set we'll hit them as hard as a Texas twister.'

Mosehan rode from Prescott at dawn the following morning, making fast time across country and calling on various friends. In each case, without telling more than necesssary to ensure co-operation he organized a passive resistance to the Syndicate.

The first result showed when Frank Ogden took his bar-tender Butch by the scruff of the neck and booted him into the street with a curt warning not to come back. Butch headed straight for the telegraph office, not seeing the two men who followed him. His message went over the wire, and he left not knowing these same two men read the copy he wrote within five minutes of his leaving. Then one turned and took up a form himself. He wrote on it and passed it to the operator who read and asked no questions. The message might appear point-less to him but he knew the Arizona Rangers always had a point to anything they did.

'Mosehan, Tucson,' it read. 'The boy was right. Pete Glendon.'

No more, no less, yet it told Captain Bertram H. Mosehan that once more Waco called the play correctly.

Butch waited for three days for some reply and finally went along to the post office once more.

'Could save your boss some money,' the old man in the post office remarked. 'That Jaqfaye *hombre* done got himself killed in a hold up.'

Butch left the room in something of a daze. The Syndicate's leaders never allowed the underlings to get close to them. Jaqfaye had been the furthest up the ladder Butch ever managed to get. Now Jaqfaye could no longer be contacted and Butch did not know how to get help to deal with Ogden. With this thought in mind he paid a visit to a rough saloon on the edge of town and selected half a dozen hard cases to help out. The saloon, like several others in Tombstone, came under the heel of the Syndicate and Butch's standing in the organisation was known. So he found little difficulty in getting the men. The difficulty started soon after.

Before Butch and his hard-case bunch could make a move they found themselves surrounded by Sheriff Behan, his deputies and two Arizona Rangers. Hauled off to jail and questioned, one of the hard-cases, wanted on charges in New Mexico, talked freely to save himself. Salvation is infectious and the other men told enough to brand Butch as being a high-up man in the Syndicate. A raid and search on Butch's room produced enough evidence to hold him for trial.

Much the same event happened in another town. Lemming, a barber, found some of his customers no longer paid their regular visits. He felt less worried about the possibility of their snubbing him than the fact that they no longer brought the money rightfully due to him as a senior member of the Syndicate. He tried to make contact with Jaqfaye and failed, then heard of the Frenchman's untimely end at the hands of a hold-up man. (Waco and Doc's story at the inquest was so convincing that Mosehan afterwards remarked Ned Buntline and Colonel Prentiss Ingraham had nothing in the story spinning line compared with the two young Texans.)

Like Butch, the barber decided on direct and independent action, hoping of rising higher in Syndicate admiration by his prompt action. He failed to achieve any more than did Butch. His hired toughs fell into the hands of the local law and once more one talked to save himself.

In these two incidents the policy of the Syndicate leaders in never hiring wanted men as their guns was justified. The two contact men, left to their own devices, took on wanted men who stood to wind up with jail terms if handed over to interested lawmen. They talked to save their own necks, or to stop themselves being shipped to the areas where their crimes brought them into conflict with the law.

A third town's contact man took warning when he heard of the death of Jaqfaye, read between the lines and tried to run out of a suddenly hostile location. He got as far as the city limits where a bullet in the back ended his flight. The killer, shot down by the following Rangers, proved to be a checker, a member of the Syndicate who watched the contact man without knowing who he contacted. This opened a new line for the Rangers to probe. They knew the checker reported but not who he reported to, only that he did not know Jaqfaye.

In three weeks the Syndicate felt the pinch. At Prescott, Waco and Doc, with Draper's help, tried to check on any man who received an unusual amount of telegraph messages, no matter how innocent they seemed. The trail seemed to point to the owner of a prosperous store which did a considerable mail order business. The store always received telegraph messages but for three weeks certain customers appeared to have been sending more than usual. That the messages were in code Waco did not doubt, but without arousing suspicion they could not check too deeply. However, Doc started to watch the owner of the business while Waco gave his attention to Counsellor Ramond Edward Hultz, the attorney who handled Jaqfay's affairs and took charge of the dead man's effects.

On the Monday of the fourth week Hultz left his large and prosperous home after dinner and strolled along the badly-lit streets. He did not see the tall young Texan who came from the shadows and walked behind him at a distance. The lawyer strode along, not leaving the better part of town and Waco followed. He expected no more than that Hultz would spend the night gambling at one of the numerous bars he attended. So it came as a surprise to Waco when the man turned and entered the gates of a church hall.

Waco crossed the street and leaned against the wall of a house, staying in the dark shadow and remaining quietly attentive. Two more men entered the same building from the window of which a light glowed behind curtains. Then a familiar shape approached and waddled up the path. Senator Thadeus Gulpe, the portly politician first met in Jaqfaye's shop who had become familiar to Waco since his arrival in Prescott. He paused at the door of the building more with the attitude of one entering a cat-house than a church hall. Seeing someone walking along the street Gulpe ducked in hurriedly.

123

Just as Waco decided he could move away and have a meal he recognized the man whose approach startled Gulpe into a rapid entry. It was the owner of the mail order house. The man turned in through the gate, strode up the path and entered the church hall. A few seconds after Doc Leroy drifted into view, walking along in an aimless idle way that would deceive an unsuspecting onlooker.

The call of a whip-poor-will brought Doc's attention to the other side of the street. He crossed and joined Waco behind the wall, only just in time as a big bulky man strode from the other direction, looked around him suspiciously, then entered the church hall.

'Know something, Doc?' Waco asked, holding his voice to hardly more than a whisper. 'I reckon we've made a hit.'

'Yeah,' agreed Doc. 'It seems tolerable strange that a man called Goldstein should be going to a church.'

Inside the small room at the rear of the church hall sat the men who ran the Syndicate, six men who had the power of life or death throughout Arizona Territory. Of them Gulpe was only a junior member, that was clear from the way the others treated him and by his scared attitude.

Gaunt as a buzzard, black-dressed and with a hard, harsh look on his face – like when he pounded the pulpit side and bellowed about the evils of strong drink at the congregation – the Reverend Arnold Postaite looked at the others. It might have been a normal stock-holders' meeting from his next actions. Taking a thick leather-bound bible from the book-shelves on the walls, Postaite ran through the accounts of the Syndicate quickly. Then he slapped the cover down and looked at the others.

'Our profits have been cut by nearly a third in three weeks. We've lost control of four towns and others are making trouble.'

'It's since Jaqfaye died and we haven't been able to ship gun-men out,' put in Gulpe, feeling as always that he would be blamed for the failure.

'You want to tell me something I don't know,' snorted Postaite, his eyes going to Hultz. 'I don't suppose you've managed to trace Jaqfaye's books and the map he kept?'

'No. I still think the Rangers opened the safe, took them and left the keys in Jaqfaye's pocket so we wouldn't be suspicious.'

'They got on to Butcher and the others too fast for just luck,' growled the big, burly man in the dress of a professional gambler, his red face turning a shade redder. 'We know that

124

the man those two Texans said killed Jaqfaye was one of our tophands. And Kinsey's not showed up again since we sent him out to kill Mosehan.'

Postaite's hand slapped hard on to the table. 'Since you, not we, sent,' he corrected angrily. 'I didn't order the killing. No, you stupid fools had to act on your own—'

'He was causing us trouble,' growled Lakeman, the gambler. 'He closed down some of our places.'

'And why?' bellowed Postaite in the tone he used when damning the sinners who drank, gambled and womanized, a tone which had rung loud and clear in a dozen towns. 'Because they couldn't stand to take a normal honest percentage but had to go all out. A blind man could have spotted the rigged decks, wheels and dice in those places. I said we ran the house games fair unless there was no chance of a come-back, but some of you had to start thinking smart—'

'Hold hard,' growled Lakeman. 'You were all for the crooked gambling factory we started in Haggertville.'

'I was. It brought in money. We supply places as far away as East Texas and north to the Idaho line. But we didn't need to ram every house we own full of it.'

'Anyway,' put in Gulpe nervously, 'It seemed like a good idea to get rid of Mosehan. He's made a lot of enemies and the Syndicate might never have been mentioned if he'd died.'

'He didn't die!' Postaite pointed out. 'Do you think everything would've been forgotten if he had died? Mosehan's important in the Territory. More, he's got loyal friends and they wouldn't rest until they found the men who had him killed. Never underestimate friends, especially the sort of friends Mosehan's kind make. He closed a few houses down but that didn't hurt us. We own in on every other place in their towns and the trade still comes to us. That should have been enough, but no. You had to try and have him killed. It failed, so most likely Kinsey and the other two are dead. But did they talk before they died?'

'Kinsey wouldn't talk,' Gulpe groaned.

'A dying man might talk,' Postaite snarled. 'Even if he didn't mean to and didn't know what he was saying.'

'Maybe you could get one of them Texans in and have him confess his sins,' sneered Lakeman who never took to the idea of being ordered about by a preacher.

Postaite sent his chair flying backwards and came to his feet. He looked as mean as a starving grizzly and a damned sight more dangerous as he leaned forward resting his palms on the top of the table. Lakeman thrust back his chair slightly but did not rise. For a moment he sat trying to act defiant then he sank down again, cowered almost. The two men in the Syndicate he most feared had been Jaqfaye and the gaunt man who was known as a sturdy hater of everything the Syndicate stood for, who preached against the evils of gambling, brothels, drinking and the other pleasures the organization catered for, the man called Postaite. Of the two Lakeman had feared Postaite the more.

'I'll not tell you again not to say those kind of things,' Postaite warned, his voice a savage hiss. He took his seat again and looked around the table, reading the fear in each face. This was why he ran the Syndicate, why he formed and made it. Early in life he learned the futility of trying to stop people having their pleasure and though he still preached against it he knew no words would ever do any good. So he took over, made the fools to whom he preached pay for their amusement. It gave him pleasure to know other men feared him.

'Now,' he went on when sure all were under his control again. 'We've got to get rid of the Rangers, or hold them off until we get organized again.'

'Who's going to call the guns together?' asked Goldstein. 'Lakeman at his saloon?'

'Can't you see that guns aren't the answer?' demanded Postaite angrily. 'We'd need more guns than we could hire to handle the Rangers, even if we could get men to chance it. We'll have to try something else.'

'Why not go to the Governor and ask him to have the Rangers disbanded?' sneered Lakeman, trying to regain his self-control.

For a moment Lakeman thought he had gone too far. The cold look ran across the preacher's face and Lakeman shuddered, expecting to be killed this time for sure. Then a savage grin came to Postaite's face, like the death sneer on the lips of a pain-wracked body.

'That's what we'll have to do. There's an election due very shortly and the Governor's more likely to be swayed by the weight of public opinion than at any other time. Suppose he received petitions for the disbanding of the Rangers?'

For a moment none of the others replied. Then Gulpe, the self-acknowledged authority on matters of public opinion and politics looked up beaming with delight.

'That's an idea,' he said enthusiastically. 'Any petition which comes in now will find itself looked over with more interest than usual. If only a small number of people from enough of the vital towns ask to have the Rangers disbanded the Governor will be forced to act. Being in politics I know—'

'You're in politics only because I let you stay in,' snapped Postaite. 'If the Syndicate didn't back you there'd be nobody fool enough to vote for you.'

Gulpe sank down into his chair a sullen look on his face and cold hate in his eyes. He and every other man of the Syndicate leaders had noticed that of late their organizer tended to look upon them less and less as partners and more as a pack of stupid underlings who hindered rather than helped him.

'All right, let's fix the details,' Postaite snapped. 'We can rely on getting a good list of names from Haggertville. But for the rest I don't know. How does our political expert think that will be?'

Hiding his resentment at the sneering tone Gulpe replied, 'It'll be a good start. But we could really do with a petition from some other town.'

'What other town can we rely on?' asked Goldstein.

'Only one,' Postaite replied. 'Prescott.'

'Here?' gasped Gulpe. 'But I don't think you could find people to sign a petition against the Rangers here.'

'We might not be able to, but Lakeman can. Every drunk, loafer, drifter and saloon hanger-on in the area will flock to his place for a free drink and willingly sign the petition to get it.'

Once more Postaite sat back and let the other men think the matter out, sure he had hit the right method. He knew that the chances of the petition bringing about a complete disbanding were slight. However, the Governor would be forced to suspend the Rangers from duty for a few weeks while the charges against them were investigated. In a few weeks the Syndicate could make fresh arrangements for the movement of their hired guns. Then they would be able to end the growing dissension in their ranks.

'That's what we'll do then,' he said, not bothering to put it up to vote as had once been the case. 'Now for this new business we were entering into. Lakeman, the man with the goods should be on his way from Mexico now. He'll deliver to you.'

'Can't say I'm too happy about that,' Lakeman growled. 'I know the penalty for what you're planning. It's heavy.'

'What risk is there?' snapped Postaite. 'The man comes, delivers the package which you record and pay him for. Then you bring it along here and I see to the distribution.'

'Is it necessary to our organization to do it, knowing the risks and the penalties?' Goldstein inquired.

127

'It is. No matter what way this business with the Rangers goes we are going to clean up our gambling houses, that means people are going to win in them. So we take in their money and pay out in ours. An easy way of spreading the money and a safe one.'

'About this petition?' the lawyer put in. 'Who'll take it before the Governor?'

'Yeah,' Lakeman agreed. 'I don't think you'll be doing it.'

'No. Hultz, Goldstein and Gulpe will hand it to the Governor and demand the inquiry. Three solid, upright and sober citizens.'

The remainder of the men gave their agreement although the three named did not appear to be any too happy about their part in the business. Not that Postaite even gave them a chance to object. He brought the meeting to a close, turned the cover of the heavy old bible over and put it with the other books on the shelf. The other men exchanged glances as they were waved from the room. In the hall they left alone but on the street Gulpe found Hultz waiting for him.

The two men walked along the street together, not noticing the shadows which now tagged along behind them. Neither spoke for a time, then Hultz glanced back over his shoulder, seeing nothing for Doc and Waco took cover in a shop doorway.

'Postaite's growing more and more abusive each time,' he said. 'We're not partners any more. He makes the decisions.'

'I've noticed that,' Gulpe replied nervously.

'I think, Senator, that the time's coming when the Syndicate needs to fold up and we make a trip to safer climes.'

Gulpe did not reply to this for a time. He thought of his bank account, his social position and the fact that they were getting in deeper water all the time. It came as something of a surprise to find another member of the Syndicate also felt the time for departure drew near.

'I thought of a trip to Europe,' Gulpe finally remarked. 'How about you?'

'The thought did occur to me,' Hultz agreed. 'We'll have to move carefully though or the rest might get suspicious.'

Neither man spoke again, both busy with their own thoughts, each trying to decide if the other would agree to a quiet betrayal which would leave their trail fairly safe. Neither decided and they separated to go to their homes where they spent a restless night trying to decide how far they should trust the other.

Waco and Doc met after seeing their men home. The two Rangers leaned against the bar on a small down-town saloon, talking in low tones and as safe as they would have been on the open range.

'Reckon we made a hit?' Doc asked.

'Likely. What better place than a church would the Syndicate find to operate from?'

'What'll we do, try to get in and find the books?'

'Nope. Let's send for Cap'n Bert, tell him what we know and see how he wants it played,' drawled Waco.

The Governor of Arizona Territory sat in his comfortable chair and held out a long sheet of paper on which appeared many names. Captain Bertram H. Mosehan took the paper and glanced at it. His face showed little change in expression but his eyes narrowed slightly as he read:

'We the undersigned, having grave concern for the manner by which the law-enforcement body known as the Arizona Rangers abuse their authority by accepting bribes, forcibly extracting confessions, murdering suspects under the guise of arresting same, and sundry other unlawful acts, do hereby petition the Governor of Arizona Territory that the Rangers be disbanded until such time as these complaints be fully investigated and legal action be taken against those responsible for the above acts!'

Under this stretched a long list of names, each with the owner's mark or signature by it.

Mosehan laid the petition on the desk and scowled at the Governor. 'You know there's not a word of truth in any of it,' he said. 'Haggertville's nothing but a hang-out for every slimy law-dodger in the Territory.'

'I know that, even though it's never been proven in a court of law. But if the opposition gets wind of it I'll have to move. So far this's the only petition I've received and I'm willing to ignore it. We both know where it's come from, or who's behind it. But, Bert, if there's another petition comes in I may have to disband you until there's been an investigation.'

Mosehan's scowl grew deeper. 'We're close, nigh on got the Syndicate treed,' he told the other man. 'That's why they're moving this way. They need time to get themselves reorganized and if you disband us they'll have that time. Then every man who shoved his neck out to help us is like to get it stomped on by some hired killer's heel.'

'I know that.'

'I passed my word that I'd stand by the folks who helped me. I'll do it even without a badge.'

'I've heard rumours there might be a petition going the rounds in Prescott,' the Governor warned. 'In fact I've a meeting with three prominent citizens tomorrow at noon. I feel you should be there. We're holding it in the private room at the Dale Hotel.'

'I'll be there,' promised Mosehan. 'I came to town because my boys have found something out and sent for me in a hurry. Got young Jed Franks along but he went downtown to see some friends. He'll be handy for producing the records for us. I'll get going now.'

'It's going to be rough, Bert,' the Governor said.

'For me – and for you,' agreed Mosehan. 'You're the man who formed us and it won't set well with folks happen they believe what's said about the Rangers.'

Mosehan left the Governor to find his two men waiting in his hotel room, or what he expected to be two men. Instead he found five Rangers, Sergeant Pete Glendon, Billy Speed and Brad Kinross having arrived while he was seeing the Governor.

'Look at this,' Mosehan told the men, passing the petition paper to Glendon.

The men gathered around to read and their comments were lurid, savage but to the point.

'I never took a bribe in my life, and I've had plenty of chances,' Glendon snapped.

'And none of us ever killed a man unless he was hidebound out to kill one of us,' Waco went on. 'The Governor doesn't believe this sort of thing, does he, Cap'n Bert?'

'He doesn't, but there'll be men who'll make political capital out of this if he lets it ride. Now I want to go extra careful around town, they might try and stir things up for us by picking fights. Where's Jed?'

'Still down town,' Waco replied. 'Sounded all-fired eager to see somebody down there.'

'So'd you if you saw the gal he's gone to see,' grinned Doc.

Mosehan repeated his warning and left the other men to go back and talk with the Governor who would call in his legal adviser to help deal with this menace to the Arizona Rangers.

'What'll we do about that petition?' Glendon asked, looking at the others. 'Wouldn't've done no good tearing it up, folks'd say it was true.'

'There's one thing we can do,' Waco replied. 'Ever heard of fighting fire with fire, Pete?'

Glendon came to his feet, a grin splitting his face. 'Yeah, I know what you mean. I'll take Billy and Brad along with me. What'll you'n' Doc be doing?'

'Checking in with the marshal. I want to know what he's heard about that petition talk in town,' Waco replied.

So the men separated at the door, but before they went their separate ways Waco made another suggestion to Glendon.

'Stay on at the post office until you get the replies.'

'Be best,' agreed Glendon. 'Keep clear of trouble if you can, boy.'

The town marshal came along the street, his stride hurried, his face showing worry. He saw the two Texans and raised a hand, calling to them.

'What's wrong, marshal?' Waco asked as they met up with Draper in the centre of the street.

'That pard of yours, young Jed Franks, he's down to the doctor's right now.'

'Jed?' growled Doc. 'What happened to him?'

Draper's eyes did not meet either man's and he felt suddenly scared, knowing the close-knit friendship of the Rangers. He knew better than try and hide something from Waco and Doc now he had told them that much.

'Somebody beat him almost to death.'

'Where?' snapped Doc.

'Who?' demanded Waco, getting to the more important aspect as far as he was concerned.

'We found him down by the Chinese laundry. One of my deputies come on him and got him to the doctor. I don't know who done it. You know how close-mouthed the Chinese are when they want to be.'

'Let's go see him,' Waco snapped.

The three men were allowed into the doctor's office. Waco and Doc went by the marshal and halted looking down at the bandage-wrapped form on the bed. The doctor joined them, pointing down.

'Whoever worked him over did a good job of it,' he said. 'Broke three of his ribs, smashed his nose, moved a few teeth. He'll live, get over it in time unless there's some permanent damage to his skull or to his sight. We don't know that until he recovers.'

Doc moved forward, gently easing the bandages away while the doctor stood back. In his time as a Ranger Doc Leroy built himself a reputation for being able to handle medical chores. Doc looked at the ugly bruises on the body and knew the marks

131

of boots when he saw them. The face carried brutal marks, signs that fists or even knuckledusters had been used.

One eye flickered open, the other puffed and swollen shut. Slowly Jed's good eye focused on the two faces before him. His crushed, bloody lips opened and he gasped, 'I never signed it.'

'What's that, boy?' Waco asked leaning closer.

'The petition, down to Lakeman's,' Jed replied, speaking awkwardly through his smashed mouth. 'They was making everybody who passed go in and sign. When I wouldn't they took me down an alley. Lakeman and two of his men. Worked me over but I wouldn't sign.'

The young man's head slumped back to the pillow again and Doc jerked his head, moving Waco away. The young Texan did not speak, but his hands clenched and he stepped back from the bed. Slowly his fingers spread and brushed the staghorn grips of his matched guns. He turned without a word and headed for the door of the office. Doc leapt forward catching Waco's arm and turning him.

'Hold hard there, boy. You mind what Cap'n Bert told you about getting into trouble until this lot's over.'

For an instant Waco's hands tensed, then relaxed. There were too many years of dangers shared and risks taken together for him to knock Doc aside as had been his first instinct. He lifted his hand, taking a small wallet from his pocket and passed it to Draper.

'Marshal, hold this. I've just resigned from the Rangers.'

'I could bring Lakeman in, Waco,' Draper pointed out.

'There's more than that to it. Lakeman knew who Jed was, still did it. That means he aims to show folks the Rangers don't mean a thing to him. I aim to show they do.'

Draper watched Waco, seeing the cold deadly glint in the blue eyes. In his time Draper had stood up and faced so-called badmen, trouble-causers on the prod and fully primed with forty-rod whisky. Yet he knew that neither he, nor any other living man, could face Waco and back him down right now. Lakeman had called the Rangers out, relying on the petition to protect him. It would hold back Mosehan and the others but not Waco. So Draper stepped back and made a mental promise that he would protect Waco from the legal consequences of his act as far as possible.

Watching the door close behind his partner, Doc made a decision. The oath of the Rangers would mean nothing if they did not all stick together. So Doc left the room and headed for the post office. He knew Waco could take care of himself and would not likely need help at first. He might later and Doc aimed to see that same help arrived when it was most needed.

Lakeman's saloon stood on Longhorn street, the largest and fanciest place in down-town Prescott. Its owner stood by the edge of the bar, a broad grin on his face as he watched the drunks and loafers from the streets signing the petition form and taking their free drinks. His eyes went to the tall, broad shouldered, curly haired man who leaned near his side.

'How about you, Bill?' he asked. 'Like to join these good citizens and get rid of the Rangers?'

Curly Bill Brocious leaned on the bar and surveyed the drunks, the tramps and the kind of men who hung around willing to do anything but work or wash. They did not look an inspiring selection of manhood to join up with. However, Curly Bill did not get a chance to put his thoughts into words for a change came in the atmosphere of the room.

The piano player, beating out a rowdy tune, suddenly brought his instrument to a jangling, discordant halt. His eyes went to the batwing doors and the tall man who stood just inside. At the bar a dirty, unshaven loafer dropped the pencil and hurriedly pushed aside the petition form, trying to look as if the last thought in his head would be to sign it. In the room every man knew of the attack on Jed Franks, knew for whom Jed worked and knew the identity of the tall, grim faced Texas boy.

'There's a bunch of yeller cur-dogs thinking of signing a petition to disband the Rangers,' Waco said, his voice carrying all around the room. 'I'm looking for them.'

A man set down his free drink untouched, moving away from the bar. He did not look at Waco as he headed for the side door. Nor did he go alone. The others, the loafers, the drifters and bag-line tramps, all had one thought in mind. Get clear of Lakeman's before Waco found their names or marks on the sheet of paper on the bar.

Inside fifteen seconds apart from Curly Brocious, Lakeman and his saloon workers stood alone. Ten men against one, eleven if Curly Bill be counted in. Yet Curly Bill, head of the Galeyville rustlers, fast gun in his own right, stood with his back to the door, leaning elbows on the bar, and smiled sardonically into his glass of whisky.

Waco moved forward, each step brushing the butts of his matched guns with eager hands. It was the walk of a killer on the prod. The saloon crowd knew the signs. The man who crossed Waco, unless he was real fast, would live no longer than a second at most.

Scooping up the petition from under the lifeless, nervously moving hand of the bartender, Waco looked at it, spat on the paper and crumpled it in his hand, tossing it at Lakeman's feet with a gesture of supreme contempt.

'Like I said, yeller cur-dogs all of them and you're the biggest of the lot, Lakeman.'

Lakeman's face lost some colour. His reputation as a hard man stood high in Prescott. He never wore a gun and never needed one while he could get in range with his hard fists or his boots. If all else failed he brought in the aid of the tough, brutal-looking bouncers who stood now in a half circle behind him.

'You've got no right to come busting in here,' Lakeman snarled. 'The Rangers've been getting away with too—'

'I'm not a Ranger any more. I resigned when I saw what you did to Jed Franks, you and some of that scum behind you.'

'Looks like you knew when to get out,' grinned Lakeman.

'Yeah. Happen I was a Ranger I'd be tied down right now. If a Ranger did what I'm going to do, your yeller pack would howl to the Governor. So I resigned from the Rangers and I'm here to tell you what I think you are. Maybe you'll not like it so when you don't just cut loose your wolf, let's hear how it howls against a man who handles a gun.'

Then Lakeman's face twisted into a sneer. He lifted the sides of his coat to show his gunless sides.

'Real brave against a man without a gun.'

Waco's lips drew back in a mirthless grin. 'You fixing to take me alone, or with two – three of your boys to help?'

'Alone, if you take off your guns.'

In this Lakeman thought he would have the edge. Few if any of the fast men he knew would risk damaging their gun hands in a fist fight and so fell easy if a man could get by their guns. He thought that blind anger and pride drove Waco to make the decision. In this Lakeman made a basic mistake. It had been several years since Waco made a move in anger and without thinking.

'Back your scum along the bar,' Waco ordered, dropping his hands towards his belt buckle but making no attempt to remove it until the order was obeyed. He watched the saloon crowd move back, passing Curly Bill who twisted around, jumped and sat with his legs swinging on the edge of the bar.

Slowly as Waco unbuckled his gunbelt Lakeman removed

his coat. He stood as tall as the young Texan and heavier in build. He tossed the coat behind him and Curly Bill caught it, resting it on his knees while his eyes took in every detail and a mocking grin came to his lips.

The gunbelt came off and Waco tossed it towards the bar. Instantly Lakeman struck. His bunched fist drove out to smash into Waco's cheek, spinning the young Texan around and sprawling him so he landed back down on a table. Lakeman flung himself forward to drive a kick between the Texan's legs that would end the fight apart from the battering. Only Waco did not stop, he went straight backwards over the table, landing on his feet at the other side and facing the charging Lakeman. Waco flung the table aside, ducking under Lakeman's blow with an ease which told he was not exactly unused to defending himself with his fists. His right smashed into Lakeman's middle, bringing a grunt of pain, the left ripped up, smashing under the saloonkeeper's jaw and staggering him.

Lakeman crashed into the bar, hung there and came off to meet Waco. Those two blows had hurt, they also gave warning that Waco was a man with whom no chances could be taken.

They met in the centre of the floor, fists lashing out and slugging home hard. For a few moments Lakeman had his own way, his extra weight counting, but he did not have the fitness of the young Texan. For him to win he must finish the fight in a hurry.

The saloonkeeper's fist smashed at the side of Waco's head, sprawling him once more on to a table. Lakeman caught up a chair and leapt forward, swinging it up and smashing it down. Waco rolled aside just in time feeling the wood splinter, the legs fly apart as the chair exploded. Then his fist slugged around, driving into Lakeman's muscle-defended belly. He heard the man's explosive grunt and lashed up a backhand blow which split Lakeman's mouth and brought blood gushing from his nose. The big saloonkeeper reeled back a few steps, pain fogging his brain for an instant. Waco drove him back with ripping, brutal blows until he hit the bar. Then Lakeman raised his foot, got it against Waco and pushed. There was brute strength in the shove, it sent Waco sprawling back, the young Texan tripped and went down, his head striking a table.

Waves of pain spun through Waco, for an instant he almost went under. Then he saw Lakeman loom above him, saw the saloonkeeper's boot driving out and rolled. Luckily Waco went far enough to avoid the main force of the kick, the boot grazed his ribs in passing and Waco's hand caught hold of a broken chair leg. Lakeman towered over Waco, on one leg, the other boot raised to stomp him. Then Waco lashed around with the chair leg, smashing it brutally against Lakeman's floor-holding leg. The pain must have been intense for the chair leg smashed full across Lakeman's shin bone; Lakeman screamed in agony, hopping back and clutching the injured limb.

Coming to his knees, shaking his head, Waco saw Lakeman attacking again, limping, pain twisting his face, but holding a bottle which he smashed against a table as he passed.

In such a fight there could be no such frills as rules of fair play. Waco knew and accepted it. He lashed out with the chair leg, smashing it with brutal force against Lakeman's arm, as it lashed towards him; The bottle fell from limp fingers and Waco drove the chair leg back, crashing it into Lakeman's belly, then as the man doubled over smashed up his knee.

Waco staggered, clutched at the side of a table, feeling as if every rib had been broken by the kick, feeling the wet stickiness of blood where the boot ripped skin from his side. He saw Lakeman hit the bar and knew he must finish the saloonkeeper fast.

Clinging to the bar Lakeman stared along it, fear in his eyes. 'Get him!' he screamed.

That was all the bouncers had been waiting for; They started to move forward to help smash the young Texan down. Curly Bill came from the bar top, landing straddle-legged before them, hands hanging thumb-hooked in his gunbelt.

'Your boss said one to one,' he reminded the men.

The bouncers halted and one of them snarled, 'Whose side are you on?'

Curly Bill's right hand dipped, steel rasped on leather and a hammer-cocking click sounded as the heavy Colt thrust under the man's nose while the savage grin came to the rustler boss's lips.

'Guess!' said Curly Bill.

Seeing no chance of getting help, Lakeman lunged along the bar to where Waco's gunbelt lay. He almost made it, hands clawing towards the staghorn grips when Waco reached him. Shooting out his right hand Waco turned the man. His left hand drove across, almost stretching Lakeman's neck three inches from the look of it. Then Waco's right hand smashed into his stomach. Lakeman hung on the bar, helpless and yet Waco did not stop. This was the yellow skunk who caused Jed Franks to be beaten within an inch of his life. Who did not have the courage to stand and fight without calling his men when he felt licked.

Through his rage Waco became oblivious to everything. He did not know the batwing doors opened and his three friends came in. Waco knew nothing until he felt himself being dragged away from Lakeman, saw the man's battered frame sliding to the floor and heard Doc's voice.

'Now easy, boy. Cool down or I'll bend a gun barrel over your fool head! Quit it afore you kill him.'

The rage left Waco slowly and he felt himself pushed down into a chair. He breathed hard and slowly his head cleared. He felt Doc touch on his ribs and then on his cheek, where blood ran from a cut over one eye.

'You got a tolerable mean temper on you, boy,' drawled Doc. 'I'd best see what I can do for him.'

Pete Glendon went towards the group of men, passing Curly Bill who had now holstered his gun again. Glendon glanced at the grinning man and said, 'Thanks, Bill, we appreciate it.' Then he looked the men over. 'I want whoever beat Jed Franks up. Which of you did it?'

Not one of the men spoke for a moment, all eyes on the stocky, hard looking Ranger sergeant. Then he stepped forward and pointed to one bouncer. Billy Speed and Brad Kinross moved in to flank Glendon.

'That one,' he said.

'Not me!'

Brutal or not the bouncer still had sense enough to know what would happen to him if the Rangers got him outside and thought he had beaten up their friend. His finger indicated two more of them.

'Take them,' Glendon snapped. 'Alive or dead, it makes no never mind to me.'

Big, rough, tough, the two bouncers had handled drunken cowhands or miners but the two men who moved in on them were cold sober and had considerable a name as being fast with their guns. So the bouncers stood while the handcuffs clicked on their wrists and then allowed themselves to be moved away towards the door.

Glendon looked around at the other men and drawled, 'There's nothing nailing you to the floor, is there?'

It might be a vague hint but it proved adequate for the needs of the recipients, for they filed out of the saloon by the side doors. Glendon turned his eyes towards the moaning saloon-keeper then went to where Waco was getting to his feet.

'You crazy Tejano,' he said, with a touch of admiration in his voice. 'You heard what Cap'n Bert had to say, didn't you?'

'I handed in my badge,' Waco answered.

'Which same you can only do to three people, Cap'n Bert, the Governor or me,' Glendon replied grimly. 'One of these days I'll get a couple of the boys and pound some sense into your fool head.'

'Say, easy now,' put in Curly Bill. 'Waco came here to arrest a suspect who attacked him first, as me'n' anybody who was here'd go in court and swear.'

'Suspect, what for?'

'Here,' Curly Bill tossed Glendon a bunch of keys and said cheerfully. 'He was after Lakeman for a safe full of forged money.'

At that moment Draper and two of his deputies arrived. Glendon and the town marshal opened the safe in Lakeman's office and lifted out a thick stack of newly minted single, five and ten dollar bills. They examined the money but neither could have sworn if the notes had been forged or if they were genuine.

'What's all this foolishness about them petitioning to disband the Rangers, Doc?' asked Curly Bill, handing Waco his gunbelt then smoothing out the crumpled paper lifted from the floor.

'The living truth,' Doc replied soberly. 'Fact being there's a meeting right now down at the Dale Hotel, demanding it. Wouldn't even wait until tomorrow.'

A grin flickered on Curly Bill's face. 'Let's take 'em this one and tell how they got it.'

Before they could leave however Glendon had stepped from the office door and came to where Lakeman slumped at a table. The Ranger sergeant grinned, flipping a bundle of money through his fingers.

'Forged. It's right easy to tell. A man'd see it from a mile off. You're under arrest, Lakeman.'

Slowly the man raised his head. Through his pain drugged mind the words penetrated and he snarled, 'Easy to tell?'

'Real easy,' scoffed Glendon. 'You'd have to be plumb loco to think you could pass that sort of rubbish off even to a booze-blinded miner.'

'The rat, the lousy, double-dealing rat!' Lakeman croaked out. 'He must've known about it!'

'Whyn't you take him along with you down to the meeting, show the Governor the sort who're starting this petition?' asked Curly Bill.

'Yeah,' said Glendon grimly. 'We'll do just that.'

Glendon caught Curly Bill's arm as they were about to follow the others out of the saloon.

'How'd you know about the money?' he asked.

'Like this, Pete. We met this *hombre* just after a bunch of Chacon's boys jumped him. Got him clear and found this money in his saddlebag. Muttered to me it was for the Syndicate and who to deliver it to. I let Turner look at it, at the Galeyville Bank and he said it was forged. So I figured to bring it here. Didn't allow it to be any of my business, I leave the Syndicate be and they don't bother me none. Then when Lakeman fixed to jump his hard boys on Waco I reckoned he wasn't the sort I'd want to tie in with. Not after he gave his word to take the boy on one to one. So I told you. Anyways, you've not a lot to complain about. Turner allowed that money was about as good as he'd ever seen.'

'It's as good as I've ever seen, too,' grinned Glendon. 'Reckon you ought to get out of town fast, Bill. Folks might get suspicious about you bringing the money.'

'There's only you and me knows, as well as Lakeman,' Curly Bill chuckled. 'Now what jury'd believe Curly Bill Brocious brought all that money here to Lakeman, even if he tells them?'

The meeting in the large private dining room at the Dale Hotel had been angry and stormy. Gulpe had called it and the Governor could not refuse.

'I think this matter must be dealt with immediately,' he said. 'A complete town give their signature to a petition, that warrants investigation. I—'

The rest of the words died as the door burst open and men entered. Gulpe stared, Hultz threw back his chair with an oath while Mosehan and the Governor came to their feet and stared as the battered Lakeman was thrust into a chair. All eyes went to Waco, seeing the marks of the fight on his face. Pete Glendon pushed to the front with Marshal Draper at his side.

'We've brought you another petition to disband the Rangers,' Glendon said quietly. 'Taken at Lakeman's saloon when one of the Rangers went to investigate a rumour that Lakeman was in possession of a quantity of forged money and to look into the attack on a man who refused to sign this same petition.'

'Those are serious charges,' Hultz snapped. 'I represent Mr. Lakeman and should have time to speak with him alone.'

Doc put the crumpled paper on the table beside the petition from Haggertville. Then to his surprise Curly Bill, having tagged along, reached out and pointed down to the Lakeman petition.

'You should see the sort of men who've been signing it. Drunks, bagline tramps, mister, you never saw such a bunch.'

'And how about you?' sneered Hultz. 'You see the kind of company the Rangers keep, Governor. This's Curly Bill Brocious, the rust—'

'Now hold hard, law wrangler,' put in Curly Bill. 'You know a man's innocent until he's proved guilty, and mister, I never been proved nothing at all.'

Which was true enough. Curly Bill and his partner Johnny Ringo might be known as rustlers but nobody had ever collected enough evidence to take them into court on a charge, much less have them convicted.

'Let's have another look at this here petition,' Curly Bill went on and picked up the Haggertville roll of names. 'Yes sir, a tolerable bunch of real fine upstanding citizens. Make a man proud to know his name was on there with them.' His fingers stabbed down on to the list. 'Take this one, Francis B. Castle, now there's a real pious name, regular church-going gent from the sound of him. Tell you something about him. He might not kill his own grandmother for five hundred dollars, but that comes as his bottom price for any other kill he makes. Then there's Barbara Martha Cousins, spinster. A kinder, more gentle old lady you couldn't ask for. Always taking in some stray to help, only it has to be a gal-stray, fairly good looking and over fifteen. That good-hearted kind lady'll take in any stray like that and never ask no more than the gal beds down with any man as comes along with the money. Well I swan, here's good ole Marshal Sam Brown signed. A pillar of honest law enforcement if ever there was one. You can't commit no crime in his town and get away with it, not until you've slipped him his right and due price for looking the other way. Yeah, that's the sort of folks on this list. I could go right through it and likely not find an honest man among them.'

'You're such a great authority on honest men,' sneered Hultz.

'Reckon I am, not being one myself. I'll tell every one of you something. If a man breaks the law and a Ranger comes after him he knows he can fight or give up. If he fights he'll likely get killed, but if he gives himself up he'll be took in fair and not mishandled any and there'll be nothing done either before or during his trial to make it worse for him.'

A knock came at the door, it opened and the old owner of

the post office came in with a sheaf of telegraph forms. He crossed to lay them on the desk and stood back with a grin.

'Thought you'd like to see these,' he said.

The Governor took up the top form and read it. 'Starting petition for the continued service of the Arizona Rangers, will send it by rider, Raines, County Commissioner, Backsight County.'

Slowly the Governor laid the form down and took up the next. He smiled and passed the forms out, every one contained much the same message. Throughout the whole of the Territory which could be reached by telegraph, messages had come to say petitions to keep the Rangers operating had been organized and would be sent.

'As Mr. Gulpe said,' the Governor remarked, leaning back expansively. 'We must go along with the majority.'

'How about Lakeman here?' asked Mosehan.

He could hardly have picked a better time. Hultz, Gulpe and the other Syndicate men were shaken by this turn of events and knew the sands were running out for them. With one accord they came to their feet intending to leave.

Lakeman saw the move and read its meaning correctly. He forced himself to his feet, pointing at them.

'Hold it, you're not getting out of this and leaving me to face it alone,' he yelled. 'They're part of the Syndicate, all three of them.'

'Shut your mouth!' Hultz bellowed, but the damage was done. He found himself surrounded by hostile men.

The four prisoners were being led to the door when Waco spoke, playing a card he hoped would take the game.

'That was a good tip the preacher gave us about the forged money,' he said loudly.

'Yeah,' Doc caught on and carried the game further. 'Pity he was leaving town when he told us, I'd like to thank him!'

That same thought hit the four men. Postaite had sold them down the river to get time to escape. With one accord and almost in the same breath all started to talk. Gulpe told the most and Mosehan looked at the Governor, ignoring the other men who had been part of the committee. For a moment the Governor nodded and Mosehan told his men to take the prisoners outside.

'And now, gentlemen,' Mosehan said quietly, turning to the men around the table. 'I'm going to tell you what I think about you and you're going to sit back and listen.'

The Reverend Postaite looked up from his desk as Mosehan entered followed by Waco. He saw Doc gently drawing the housekeeper back from the room, then step in and close the door. For all that he gave no sign of guessing what the action meant.

'Well, gentlemen?' he said. 'What can I do for you?'

'We'd like to take a look in that bible, the big one on the shelf,' Mosehan replied. 'We've a search warrant.'

'Go ahead.'

Postaite came to his feet, hands gripping the edge of the table as he spoke. He gave a sudden heave, throwing the table over, at the same moment his left hand whipping under his arm, bringing out a Merwin & Hulbert pocket revolver from a shoulder clip. The move was fast and showed long hours of practice. Waco thrust Mosehan to one side not an instant too soon. Postaite's first shot cut the air just where the Ranger Captain's body had been an instant before. Hurriedly the man tried to correct his aim but Doc Leroy's Colt rocked back against his palm. Postaite spun around, staggered and went down, the gun falling from his hand. He clawed at it but Waco sprang forward and kicked it from under his hand. Doc hostered his Colt to move forward while Mosehan turned and kept the screaming housekeeper outside as his men, with the town marshal, rushed the building.

'Not much chance, is there, Ranger?' croaked Postaite.

'Not much,' Doc replied.

'I suppose somebody talked, Gulpe most likely. I've been riding them a bit hard these last few weeks. You'll find everything in the bible. They'll be some folks buying trunks real soon.

'Why'd you do it?' Waco asked. 'Heard you preaching one time as I passed the church and you sounded tolerable against everything your bunch ran.'

Postaite looked at Waco, a grin twisting his lips. He allowed Doc to make him more comfortable but refused offered tending of his wound.

'It'll only make it linger a while,' he said. 'Why'd I do it, Ranger? I used to preach against gambling, drinking and all the rest. Folks came along, they would listen and drop a dime or so in the collection box, then spend a pile of dollars on the things I preached against. There didn't seem any point in my carrying on. So I picked men and started the Syndicate. We grew fast and big but more and more I found I and I alone ran the organization. More and more it fell on me to plan. I think I pushed the others too hard these last few months. I had the power to do it, they knew and hated me for it. Then you came along. In a few weeks you broke down the organization it took nearly ten years to build. There's a moral in it somewhere I suppose. Perhaps you could find a better preacher than me to make it.'

Mosehan stood at the table looking through the book. In it was all he needed to smash the Syndicate for ever. He closed the book and looked to where Doc drew Postaite's eyelids over dead eyes.

'Gone, huh?' he asked.

'Sure,' Doc replied.

'It's maybe as well. Word'll be out now and some of them'll run, get clear,' said Mosehan. 'We can't help that. Anyway the tricks you bunch pulled to make Lakeman talk'd likely take some explaining away in court. Might some of them even get off, but with this book I don't reckon they can. It won't matter if they do.' He waved his hand to the dead man on the floor. 'When you stomp on a snake's head and crush it you've got a tolerable dead snake and a dead snake's not dangerous any more.'

CHAPTER FOUR

THE END

'LET me go instead of you!'

Captain Bertram H. Mosehan looked at Waco and a half smile played on his lips as he replied, 'You've asked that fifty times at least, boy, but the answer's still the same. No.'

'It's not fitting you should go,' growled Waco, looking at his partner, Doc Leroy for support. 'Is it, Doc?'

'It's surely not,' agreed Doc, rolling a smoke with some distaste as if the smell of tobacco held no pleasure for him any more.

Mosehan looked them over with pride in his eyes. They were a pair to draw and a man could be proud to merely know them. Mosehan did more than know them, he had their unswerving loyalty and knew they were worried about the mission he set himself to do. Their present concern for his well-being touched him more than he cared to admit.

'Look, you pair of wet-hens,' he said quietly. 'I've told you both, and all the other boys, that I'm handling this chore, and why I'm doing it. For one thing it's breaking the law, not just our law, but international law as well. If the man doing it gets caught below the border he'll be lucky if they do no more than shoot him. That's why I've got to be the one to do it. I don't even know how far I can trust Stiles or Alvord.'

Crossing the room Waco looked to where a sullen-looking young man sat by the corral and moodily whittled at a stick.

'That's why I reckon you need at least one of us along. To hell with any kind of law I say.'

'Hell of a thing for a duly sworn-in lawman to say,' grunted Mosehan, not losing his patience at the insistence of the two men. 'No go, either of you. I've made my deal with Burt Alvord and I'll see it through. He said he'd set Chacon up for me but that I'd have to go in alone and take him.'

'Which same's why I don't like it,' Waco answered. 'We all

know Stiles and Alvord've rode with Chacon and it was Alvord who got Chacon out of Tombstone jail when they had him.'

'Sure. And now Alvord's wanting to come in without having some sheriff or other working him over with a belt to make him tell where the stageline's money's hid out. Alvord knows I want Chacon, not the money.'

Waco and Doc knew all this, knew it and did not like it. Since breaking the Syndicate, Mosehan found stronger political opposition than ever to himself and his men. A number of people lost good friends in the clean-up following the killing of the Syndicate's head and the producing of his books. So Mosehan handed in his resignation, allowing another man to take over command of the Rangers and keep them going. Then Mosehan accepted the Governor's request that he made a final try at either catching or killing Augustino Chacon, the famous *Peludo*, the Hairy One. Chacon, the most ruthless, deadly and cold-blooded of all the Mexican *bandidos,* a man with at least twenty-nine murders to his credit, stood alone at the peak of his kind. He struck like a stick-teased rattler, killed without second thoughts and when chased, fought off pursuit until he was below the Mexican line and safe for no man could be extradited from his own country.

That Mosehan agreed to stay on said much to commend him for he had offers of more lucrative and far safer work in his pocket; managing cattle ranches which had been his life's work until forming the Rangers. Now he planned to play a desperate game in order to bring the arch-murderer to justice.

Yet there was a fly in the ointment. Chacon was safe from extradition and not even the gentlemen's agreement between Mosehan and Emilo Kosterliski, head of the *Guardia Rurale* of Mexico, by which wanted men from either nation could be passed over the border to their own country for arrest, counted. Chacon, a Mexican, never committed any crime below the border, so he could not be touched by the *Rurales.* This meant ordinary methods of arrest would not work and what Mosehan planned would give the politicians a field day against him.

The chances of catching Chacon on American soil were not great, less since he heard Mosehan was after him and announced that he aimed to stay below the border for a time. So Mosehan aimed to go and bring Chacon out by force. This amounted not only to kidnapping but also to breaking international law, although once Chacon found himself in an American court he would never escape alive.

To help bring in Chacon the aid of two wanted men, Billy Stiles and Burt Alvord, became necessary. Both were friends with the Mexican and trusted by him. Yet Alvord wished to hand himself over to the law. He and Stiles, aided by two more men, robbed a stage in Arizona, getting a large amount of money being shipped to pay mine workers. By a trick Alvord later hid the money, then a slip made him run for the line. His only chance of ever seeing the loot again would be to come back, face trial, do his time and then collect. However, with a large reward for the recovery of the money at stake, the various lawmen in the hunt would be inclined to take painful measures to make Alvord reveal its hiding place. Alvord did not like the idea of being subjected to whippings and other measures of persuasion likely to be used by some law enforcement bodies. So he made a deal with Mosehan; Chacon for safe conduct to some big town jail in which he could stay safe from harsh treatment until placed on trial.

Mosehan tried to arrange all this in secret but Jed Franks, over his beating, was back at work and learned enough to make him warn the other members of the Rangers. Mosehan found himself with a mutiny brewing and to prevent himself having every Ranger on hand agreed to take two to the rendezvous by the border. Mosehan had more than a strong suspicion Waco and Doc made use of their knowledge of crooked gambling in the card drawing to select the two men who accompanied him.

So they were now in a small cabin by the border, one of the string of such places built and maintained by the outlaws who rode the trails which began north in the Hole-in-the-Wall and Robbers' Roost country of Wyoming. Here the Rangers stayed until Alvord brought them word of where Chacon would be.

'Hoss coming, Cap'n Bert,' Waco spoke from the window, looking towards the Mexican line. 'That damned Billy Stiles never said a word about it.'

The three men stepped from the cabin and halted in the shade of the porch while Billy Stiles, dressed in his cheap copy of a range country dandy's dress, rose, tossed aside the stick, closed his knife and looked towards the approaching rider.

Burt Alvord rode slouched in his saddle, looking round shouldered and mean as a buzzard. He wore the dress of a Mexican vaquero, but the low tied guns at his sides hung in a western style belt and holsters. He halted his horse, shifty eyes going to Waco and Doc, then around him as if he contemplated flight.

'Shouldn't be but you'n Billy here, Cap'n,' he said sullenly.

'You can trust these boys like you can trust me,' Mosehan replied. 'I reckon you've fixed something up for me by now?'

Alvord scowled, never relaxing for a minute. 'Chacon'll be at that spring I showed you, alone. I fixed that. He allows we aim to buy a bunch of horses you stole only don't want his bunch to share in the profits. You 'n' Billy can go down there and take him. I'll stay on here.'

'That wasn't the arrangement,' growled Waco.

'Neither was having you pair here,' put in Stiles, getting up courage now his pard had arrived.

'It's that way or not at all,' Alvord went on, ignoring Stiles.

Thinking how typical of the way Alvord worked this was Mosehan agreed. The dark outlaw never took a chance if he could help it. Even the robbery was performed by Stiles and another man, Alvord reserving himself for the risky business of taking the loot and hiding it after the robbery had been safely accomplished. Now not even the other three members of the gang knew where to find the loot.

'Let's ride,' Mosehan said.

After saddling Mosehan's horse, Waco and Doc stood back, watching their leader and waited for him to ride out with Stiles and Alvord. Mosehan came to the two Texans and looked hard at Waco.

'Now listen to me, boy,' he said. 'You're an accessory before and after the act in this thing, you and Doc both. When I come back we'll all have to get out of sight for a spell or we'll wind up in jail. We only need to have Chacon delivered safe to get him tried and hung, so we can go when we've done it. But I'm not having you any deeper in this thing. Understand?'

'Yeah.'

'Then you'll stay here for four days. Happen I'm not back by then I won't be coming and you can go to tell the Governor so.'

'Me'n Doc could maybe trail along well back—'

'No. That's an order, boy. Doc, if he tries to follow me shoot him in the leg. I'm asking your word not to follow me, boy.'

For a long moment Waco did not reply. Then he nodded. 'You've got my word. But if you don't get back in four days, let the Governor worry, I'm going to get hold of Dusty, Mark and the Kid and we're coming down there to make sure Chacon pays.'

'What riles me is them stinking politicians who'd jail you for

147

fetching a murdering rat like Chacon back the only way you could,' Doc went on.

'That's life's rich pattern, Doc,' grinned Mosehan and swung into his saddle.

Waco went to where Billy Stiles stood ready to mount his horse. The young man tried, and failed, to meet Waco's cold stare and began to turn. Out shot Waco's hand, catching him by the sleeve and spinning him around. Then Waco's hand bunched in Stiles' vest, lifting him and thrusting him into the corral fence.

'Listen good to me, Billy,' said Waco, his voice hardly more than a whisper yet Billy Stiles never forgot it. 'Happen you sell out Cap'n Bert just put your Colt's nose in your mouth and drop the hammer, then bury yourself, 'cause the world won't be big enough for you to run from me in.'

Doc came forward fast. 'Let him go, boy!' he barked. 'Do it or so help me I'll put that bullet in your leg right now.'

Waco shoved Billy Stiles back with a contemptuous gesture and stepped back. Doc looked Stiles over, his cold eyes seeming to burn into the outlaw's brain and kick at his nerves.

'Like Waco said, Billy,' Doc drawled easily. 'Happen you leave Cap'n Bert in bad just pray the boy gets you afore I do. I know some good ways of making a man die and making it hurt bad. And I can do them so they look like accidents.'

Billy Stiles tried to meet the cold eyes of the two Texans and failed once more. With a snarl that sounded more like the whine of a whipped puppy he turned to swing into the saddle of his horse. Riding after the other two men Stiles felt as if a cold hand kept running along his spine. He felt afraid and not just of the two Texans' guns. The way they looked at him, those cold unfeeling eyes, put the fear of God into him for he knew Waco and Doc meant every word they said.

Waco and Doc watched the three men ride towards the ridge which in these parts showed the border with Mexico. Then they turned and walked back into the hut. Waco flung his hat across the room in a gesture of disgust. He began to curse the politicians, doing it fluently and comprehensively.

'Why in hell didn't Cap'n Bert let us trail him?' he finally asked bitterly.

'Didn't want us to get in any deeper than we are now,' Doc answered. 'He's risking jail at best, a bullet if the Mexican army sees him or worse if Chacon gets suspicious and has his bunch around. Then when he gets back that lousy bunch at Prescott are going to scream for his hide for what he's done and Sam

Strogoff's Pinkertons'll jump at a chance to move in and take him – and you.'

'I'd lose sleep worrying over what Pinkertons could do to me,' growled Waco.

'Reckon you would. Cap'n Bert's a good man, too good for the lousy deal he's getting.'

'Sure,' agreed Waco. 'Happen I'd had choice he's the man I'd take for a father.'

So Captain Bertram H. Mosehan rode to the south, rode to break the law and bring in the most dangerous *bandido* of them all. He knew he went with his life balanced on the thin edge of a real sharp razor. One slip, one hint of anything going wrong would see both Alvord and Stiles desert him at best, throw in with and help Chacon at worst. All which stood between Mosehan and a most unpleasant death was his courage, gun skill and the greed of Burt Alvord.

About three miles below the border Alvord drew his horse to a halt and lifted a hand to point away into the distance.

'That's where you'll find him, Cap'n. Down there camped by a spring either tonight, tomorrow or the next night, I'm not sure when he'll make it. Now I'll head back over the border and meet your man.'

Mosehan shook his head, a cold grin coming to his face. 'Pete Glendon won't make a move until he gets word from me. I told him to wait until I send word Chacon was over the border before he took you in. Know something, Burt. Happen I don't make it back I'd be real unsurprised if Pete and the boys didn't turn you over to Strogoff and his crowd, despite my orders.'

Alvord snarled out a curse but knew he could not argue. He knew Mosehan had kept his word. He also knew the other Rangers would disobey orders if their leader did not return and they suspected treachery on Alvord's part.

'I told you Chacon'll be alone down there. He doesn't want to share with the rest of his men. Things've been a mite tight down here since he stopped raiding up north of the border and he needs the money. You'll get him all right.'

'Then you'll have nothing to worry about. See you, Burt.'

'Yeah, see you, Cap'n,' Alvord replied. 'You help the Cap'n all you can, Billy. See you do.'

In view of the way Stiles allowed Alvord to trick and use him it could be assumed he was far from being intelligent. However he could feel that the game had gone beyond the depths he liked to be at. Something told him he was being used again and the odds were high. His eyes went to the distance where the spring lay hidden in a fold of the ground. He began to consider his fate if anything went wrong with the capture of Chacon. Stiles had spent time around the Chacon camp and seen the sheer brutality the Mexican and his men practised as casually as other men laughed and joked. He thought also of the words of the two Texans. Whichever way the game went Billy Stiles knew he would be real unpopular and make some bad enemies.

Guessing what preyed on Stiles' mind, Mosehan rode slightly behind the young outlaw and watched him. Mosehan glanced at the sky and estimated how much time he had before dark. He decided not to reach the spring until after dark and so told Stiles to stop and rest the horses.

Neither man spoke as they sat in the shade of a bush and smoked, waiting for the sun to go down. Then Stiles settled down using his arms for a pillow and shut his eyes as if going to sleep. Mosehan took the hint, also settling down, drawing his hat over his face a little and lay still, breathing evenly. For almost half an hour neither man moved, then Stiles stirred and peered towards Mosehan. Slowly the young outlaw eased himself into a sitting position and spoke quietly.

'Cap'n Mosehan?'

Satisfied that Mosehan really was asleep Stiles came to his feet and padded silently towards his horse. He kept a wary eye on Mosehan all the time and on reaching his tethered horse cautiously opened the saddlebag, slid in a hand then took out a pair of handcuffs, relics from the days before the robbery when he and Alvord were deputy sheriffs. Stiles threw a look at Mosehan who still lay as if asleep. Then he opened the handcuffs and swung one down, allowing it to click closed around his wrist. He removed the handcuff and began to move slowly towards Mosehan.

With a grunt and a groan Mosehan came awake, stirring first and causing Stiles to whip the handcuffs into his trousers pocket fast. Then Mosehan sat up, stretched and came to his feet.

'Something wrong, Billy?'

'Naw, Cap'n. Just went to see if the hosses are all right. Be night by the time we get to the spring.'

For all that Mosehan did not appear to be in any hurry to start. He insisted they ate some food from his saddlebags and drank water from their canteens. Then they mounted and rode on. The sun set and through the darkness Mosehan saw a small, flickering camp fire in the hollow a mile ahead.

A slim, tall and lithe figure rose from by the fire at the approach of the two riders. His right hand dipped, a Smith & Wesson revolver slid into his palm in a very fast move.

'*Quien es?*'

'Stiles and the *hombre* Burt sent,' Stiles replied in a loud voice as if making sure there could be no mistake. '*Saludos,* Augustino!'

Mosehan looked for the first time at the man he sought, the most wanted murderer in the Rangers' book. Chacon stood six foot, his lean frame showed a whipcord strength and power. The beard which gave him the name of the Hairy One had been shaved off, leaving a lean, handsome, yet hard and merciless face. His clothes were silver decorated and expensive, the dress of a rich *hidalgo,* but the gunbelt, into the holster of which he returned the pearl-handled Smith & Wesson, showed signs of use and the knife at the other side was no decoration.

Even though he had holstered his gun, Chacon gave no sign of relaxing. The wolf caution which kept him alive did not desert him even when safe below the border. He studied the two men for a moment, then said:

'Leave your horses over there and join me.'

Mosehan looked around him. One thing was for sure, Chacon picked this place real good. They were surrounded by scrub-oaks through which silent passage would be difficult and offering them cover from prying eyes. Unless Chacon's men were already in place they could not get close without giving warning. Then Mosehan saw another way of looking at the rendezvous. If he himself had men following they could not move in without alerting Chacon and none could see from the rims of the hollow just who stood at the fire. It began to appear that Alvord told the truth and Chacon did plan to double-cross his men.

They gathered at the fire and squatted on their haunches around it. Chacon's eyes went to Mosehan; cold eyes, black and unfeeling as those of a diamondback rattlesnake.

'I hear you have horses for sale. It is strange, I have heard nothing of a herd being – bought, shall we say?'

Mosehan tried to look as easy as he felt uneasy. 'Hell, that was up towards Backsight, got them from Colonel Raines' hoss spread. That's well north of where you ride. You got friends up there?'

'I have friends in many places. They hear much and from them I hear.'

Deciding the only way would be to act as a tough and touchy

151

horse-thief whose word had been doubted Mosehan gave an angry grunt.

'Billy Stiles here brought me and Burt Alvord vouched for me. If that's not good enough I'll find me another buyer.'

Chacon laughed, a hard, brittle and savage laugh. 'You would've been dead if you came without their vouching for you, señor. I am very fast with a gun.'

Coming to his feet in a casual move and keeping his hand clear of his gun, even though Chacon's eyes went to his face and the Mexican tensed like a crouching cougar, Mosehan turned and walked towards his horse. At any moment he expected to feel the shattering impact of a .44 bullet between his shoulders but kept his step firm and did not even glance back. His rifle hung in the saddleboot of the horse but he ignored it, reaching instead into the saddlebag and taking out a bottle of whisky. Then he walked back to the fire, meeting Chacon's gaze all the time.

'Here, let's have a drink,' he said, removing the cork and holding out the bottle to Chacon. 'This's the best whisky you'll ever taste.'

'You first, señor,' Chacon replied. 'An old custom of my country.'

Feeling he had never needed a drink more in his life, Mosehan tilted the bottle and felt the harsh bite of the whisky as it slid down his throat. He wiped the top of the bottle and passed it to Chacon who accepted, sniffed at the bottle then drank. Chacon appeared to relax slightly when he tossed the bottle into Stiles' eager and nervous hands.

'The good Billy appears unduly worried, señor,' Chacon remarked with a grin. 'He is not used to a life of crime of course.'

'Likely get used to it, running with Burt,' Mosehan replied, slapping at his pockets. 'Hell, I'm out of tobacco. Either of you gents got any?'

For all his faults Chacon could show all the social graces, even the unwritten kind of the range country. He removed a small case and held it to Mosehan who accepted one of the thin black cigars. Chacon took another and then offered Stiles the case.

Mosehan drew in a deep breath. This was the chance, the moment. He reached down and took a twig from the fire with his left hand, casually holding it out to Chacon. The Mexican nodded his thanks, bent forward to take the offered light – and needed to take his eyes from Mosehan for a second or so.

It was enough!

Mosehan's hand dipped, the Peacemaker slid from his holster and the hammer drew back with a satisfying click.

'Throw up your hands, Chacon. I'm Captain Mosehan of the Arizona Rangers.'

Without as much as moving an inch Chacon coolly surveyed the bore of the big Colt which lined on him. Slowly he came to his feet trying to stare Mosehan down for the vital split second he needed to have a chance at making his draw and beating the drop. He held his hands away from his sides, clear of his weapons but did not raise them higher.

'What difference will raising my hands make?' he asked. 'You could kill me just as easily with them raised as lowered.'

Even now all could go wrong and Mosehan knew it. A split second's inattention would be enough to let Chacon make his move. Mosehan had seen the way the Mexican drew and knew that, if not among the ten fastest guns, Chacon could still move fast enough to chance beating the drop.

'All right, Stiles,' Mosehan snapped. 'Handcuff him.'

'H-handcuff?' gulped Stiles. 'W-where do I get the cuffs from?'

'Out of your pocket, you double-dealing rat,' replied Mosehan, his voice savage. 'I wasn't asleep and saw you fooling with them.'

Gulping down something which seemed to be blocking his throat Stiles moved towards Chacon. He was still not fully committed to either side and there might be a chance of making some definite move which would allay Chacon's suspicions.

'From behind, not between us,' Mosehan barked. 'You've held a law badge and know the right way.'

Chacon tensed slightly as Stiles moved behind him. Seeing this, Mosehan decided a warning would not be amiss.

'When you raided Morenci and killed the storekeeper, Chacon, I made a promise that I'd hang your hide on the wall. That storekeeper you and your boys cut up was my friend. I aim to take you across the border alive, or leave you here – dead.'

The *bandido* nodded, knowing Mosehan was not bluffing this time. He submitted to having his hands secured by the handcuffs for Mosehan moved around to be able to see that Stiles did his work correctly. Stiles realized he had fully committed himself now. Chacon would never believe he brought the handcuffs along for any other purpose than their present use. He removed the fancy Smith & Wesson, tossing it to one side, then slid the knife from its sheath and flung it away into the bushes. With the air of one who had done his work well Stiles stepped clear. Then he gave a startled yelp as he saw the bore of the Colt turn towards him.

'Hey Cap'n!' he squawked. 'You're pointing that thing at me!'

'That's right,' Mosehan replied with a cold grin. 'Shed the gunbelt and toss it this ways.'

Chacon laughed. 'You trust the good Billy, no?'

'I trust the good Billy no,' admitted Mosehan. 'Which same I reckon I showed more sense than you did.'

Opening his mouth to protest his good intentions Billy Stiles unbuckled his gunbelt. He saw the angry gleam in Mosehan's eyes and knew the Ranger Captain's temper was wearing thin. Under the strain a lesser man might have lost his head by now and thrown lead into both Stiles and Chacon. So Stiles obeyed the order to toss aside his gun.

Without holstering his Colt, Mosehan moved around to collect all the weapons. He picked up Chacon's revolver and Stiles' gunbelt, placing the first in his saddlebag and the second around his saddlehorn. Then he glanced at the rifles in the saddleboots of Chacon's big grulla horse and Stiles' fast little bay. Holstering his Colt as he drew Stiles' rifle Mosehan worked the lever fast, throwing the bullets out until the magazine tube held no more. Then he shoved the rifle back and took the Centennial Model Winchester from Chacon's saddle and emptied it. He slid the rifle back, watching the others. That rifle would be a vital piece of evidence against Chacon for it came from the store in Morenci, taken from the murdered storekeeper.

While all this happened Chacon watched and calculated his chances. He might have tried to turn and dash for the cover of the scrub oaks. But he remembered how fast Mosehan threw down on him. Before he could take two steps he would be dead. So he stayed still, knowing that while alive he had a chance of escape.

'What now, *señor*?' Chacon asked.

'We wait for daylight and ride for the border,' Mosehan replied. 'So sit down. Stiles, tend to the horses.'

Chacon settled down while Billy Stiles took care of the horses. Mosehan moved back until in a position where he could watch both men. Chacon sat comfortably and his face showed nothing of his thoughts. He estimated the distance to the border and the chance of meeting some of his men or other friends before reaching it.

'I don't think Colonel Kosterliski would be eager to see you kidnapping a Mexican citizen, *señor*,' he finally said. 'I have heard the *Rurales* are in this part of the border. That is why I chanced coming here.'

'Yeah, that's what Don Emilio wanted folks to think. Keep your *amigos* out of my way. I saw him a week back. He wouldn't help me take you, but he took all his men west and won't be back for a few days.'

An admiring gleam showed in Chacon's eyes. He could admire a shrewd enemy and a brave one. The Ranger Captain proved to be both and Chacon bore him no malice, reserving that for Billy Stiles and Burt Alvord.

'I wish you every success in your plan, Captain. It will be a pity after all your work to die with me uncaptured.'

Saying that Chacon lay down on his side, ignoring the awkwardness of having his hands fastened behind his back and went to sleep. Stiles also settled down but Mosehan rested his back against a tree and watched them. Three times in the night Chacon woke and looked towards Mosehan but each time the Ranger Captain's eyes showed he did not sleep.

At dawn Mosehan roused the other two and ordered Stiles to saddle the three horses ready to ride. With a moan but without argument Billy Stiles did as ordered. He tried no tricks and stood back when the horses were saddled, a pained look on his face as Mosehan tested that he could mount without the saddle slipping and throwing him to the ground.

Next Stiles helped Chacon mount for Mosehan took no chances and made the man keep his handcuffs on. Mosehan drew his rifle, throwing a bullet into the breech then took a length of strong but thin cord from his saddlebag. First he fastened one end around the muzzle of his rifle, just behind the foresight, tossed the other end to Stiles and ordered him to fasten it around Chacon's waist.

With the order obeyed Mosehan mounted his horse, sitting it behind Chacon's while the Mexican twisted around to look at him. The cord hung between them, not too tight but sinister in its purpose.

'Listen good to me, Chacon,' Mosehan said quietly. 'I'm riding right behind you and my finger'll be on the trigger of the rifle. If you go out of the saddle or I get shot I'll fall, that cord won't break and it'll keep the rifle lined on you. This rifle's set with a hair-trigger so you know what'll happen?'

'I know.'

For all his position Chacon admired the cold, deadly smart

155

way in which the Ranger Captain handled the situation. No matter which way he tried to throw himself from his horse, if he tried to make the horse escape even, he would draw the barrel of the rifle after him like it was magnetized to him and the finger on the set-trigger would close, firing the bullet even without need for Mosehan to aim it.

Riding ahead of the other two, Billy Stiles tried desperately to decide on his best course of action. No matter what happened now Chacon would never forgive him for bringing the head of the Arizona Rangers to the meeting. Chacon's many friends were likely to be looking for blood when they heard of his part in the capture of the *bandido*. They would look for Billy to get revenge. Yet if he helped Chacon escape and the *bandido* excused his part in the capture there would still be those two deadly young Texans and the friends they could gather. One way or another Billy Stiles' future looked black indeed.

The cross-country ride, with the capture of Chacon, had seldom been matched and never bettered in the annals of enforcement. Alone, hindered rather than helped by the men supposed to be siding him, Mosehan went into Chacon's own country and arrested him. Took the most deadly killer of them all from an area where Chacon held power even over such law as there was. Brought his prisoner back when at any moment friends of the *bandido* might see them and cut in for the same friends knew the country far better than Mosehan did.

The sun had long passed noon when they rode towards the shack on the United States side of the border. Chacon sat lounging in his saddle. He only spoke once during the ride.

'I hope, *señor*,' he said as they approached the border, 'That you know you are breaking international law by kidnapping a Mexican citizen and taking him over the border.'

'Reckon I do,' Mosehan agreed.

With that they rode on again, in silence. Chacon's eyes went to the big paint and black horses in the corral and he felt that there might be a chance for he knew the usual occupants of the shack to be long-riding outlaws.

The delight died when the two men came from the shack, both raising their hands in greeting.

'Yahoo!' howled Waco. 'You got him, Cap'n Bert.'

Doc's wild cowhand yell shattered the air as he bounded forward to meet their leader and the prisoner. He grinned at Mosehan who slid down from the horse and removed the cord from the rifle barrel. Then Doc gripped Mosehan's hand hard, the look in his eyes telling Mosehan more than any words how he felt.

Waco moved forward, throwing a glance at the unarmed Stiles. 'Hopes ole Billy behaved himself.'

' 'Bout as well as could be expected. Get Chacon in the shack.'

Handing his gun to Waco as a simple precaution Doc moved forward and helped the *bandido* dismount. Then Doc stepped clear and Chacon shrugged. Escape did not seem very likely now, watched by three obviously capable men.

The prisoner allowed himself to be taken into the shack, his handcuffs removed only after leg irons clamped on his ankles. He showed no concern, making small talk, finding that he and Waco had a mutual acquaintance in the Ysabel Kid. Doc looked at Mosehan who prepared to catch up on his missed sleep.

'We'll take him to Solomonsville in the morning. Then I'll run him to Prescott by stage and after that we'd best scatter.'

'That riles me,' Doc replied. 'You've done what the sheriffs, U.S. marshals, Pinkertons and the Yankee cavalry couldn't do and now you're on the run for it. I wish some of those lousy politicians had been here on the border when Chacon raided. They wouldn't be so all-fired eager to talk then.'

'That would have pleased me also,' Chacon put in dryly. 'If I had killed them they wouldn't have forced Captain Mosehan to act as he did.'

The following dawn Mosehan and his men escorted their prisoner to Solomonsville and the stageline. Billy Stiles, turned free, headed north, following the old owlhoot trail until beyond Utah, then pushing into the sparsely populated lands to the north-west where he spent the rest of his life under an assumed name.

At Solomonsville Mosehan had a stroke of luck. Ned Draper, town marshal of Prescott, was on the stage with two deputies, returning from delivering prisoners to Yuma penitentiary. With such an escort Mosehan did not need to delay his two young friends any more.

'It's been good knowing you pair of hellers,' he said. 'Tom Rynning told me that he'd have you back as soon as this blows over.'

'Likely, but like we told him, it won't make his work any easier,' Waco replied. 'Nope, we'll split up for a spell. Doc's heading over to see Stone Hart and the boys at the Wedge and I'm going visiting up to Backsight.'

The driver of the coach showed signs of wishing to leave. Mosehan gripped each hand hard, tried to speak, but he could not get the words out. His hand tingled from the powerful grip of the tall boy whose only name was Waco.

'See you down trail sometime,' he finally said, using the old cattle-drive farewell. With that Mosehan climbed into the coach and it lurched forward taking him out of Waco and Doc's life.

'There goes a real good man,' Waco said quietly. 'See you in a couple of months, Doc. We'll head on back to Texas, start work for Ole Devil again.'

Mosehan delivered his prisoner and then carried on east. When the trial opened the defence counsel tried to have him produced to explain how a Mexican citizen came to be kidnapped and brought over the border. The politicians yelled and raved but public sympathy stood firm against them. Their efforts to have Mosehan found and brought to trial came to nothing for suddenly sheriffs, U.S. marshals, town marshals and Captain Rynning's Rangers found themselves too busy to look. Only the Pinkertons might have searched, but a large-scale robbery came and threw most of their men into the hunt for the robbers.

Gone without trace also were the two young Texans who helped Mosehan. Here Strogoff of Pinkerton's insisted on sparing a man for he hated Waco bitterly. Backsight would be the most likely place for Waco and Strogoff sent a man there.

On the day Chacon entered the dock on trial and admitted proudly his identity, Waco sat his horse looking towards the junction of the Colorado and San Juan Rivers and the town which lay between them. He left Backsight rather than involve his friends in any trouble, riding north across the Utah line.

'Looks like a fair-sized town, lots of folks always coming and going, ole Dusty hoss,' he said. 'Let's ride in and see, shall we?'

The big paint stallion snorted and started forward. Waco studied the saloon which lay at the point just where two bridges crossed the rivers.

'Yes sir, a real nice town. One thing's for sure, Dusty hoss. We've done with law work now.'

Saying this Waco rode by the sign which announced the town of Two Forks.

THE COLT AND THE SABRE BY J. T. EDSON

The Confederate Army needed arms. They knew where the arms were to be had, but payment in gold was necessary and gold was short in the South.

Belle Boyd, beautiful Confederate spy, knew how to get the gold but needed help if her plan was to succeed.

Fate threw her in with a certain captain in the Texas Light Cavalry – a young man who was already spoken of in the same breath as the legendary leaders of the South.

His name was Dusty Fog.

0 552 08017 9   45p

A SELECTED LIST OF CORGI WESTERNS FOR YOUR READING PLEASURE

J. T. EDSON

☐ 07991 X	THE HOODED RIDERS No. 21	*J. T. Edson* 45p
☐ 08011 X	THE BULL WHIP BREED No. 22	*J. T. Edson* 45p
☐ 08017 9	THE COLT AND SABRE No. 26	*J. T. Edson* 45p
☐ 08020 9	COMANCHE	*J. T. Edson* 45p
☐ 08241 4	THE FORTUNE HUNTERS No. 47	*J. T. Edson* 40p
☐ 08279 1	SIDEWINDER No. 52	*J. T. Edson* 40p
☐ 08706 8	SLIP GUN No. 65	*J. T. Edson* 40p
☐ 08783 1	HELL IN THE PALO DURO No. 66	*J. T. Edson* 40p
☐ 09650 4	YOUNG OLE DEVIL No. 76	*J. T. Edson* 40p
☐ 09905 8	GET URREA! No. 77	*J. T. Edson* 40p

LOUIS L'AMOUR

☐ 09849 3	SACKETT'S LAND	*Louis L'Amour* 40p
☐ 09354 8	LANDO	*Louis L'Amour* 40p
☐ 09353 X	RADIGAN	*Louis L'Amour* 40p
☐ 09352 1	THE BURNING HILLS	*Louis L'Amour* 40p
☐ 09351 3	CONAGHER	*Louis L'Amour* 40p
☐ 09350 5	THE LONELY MEN	*Louis L'Amour* 40p
☐ 09343 2	DOWN THE LONG HILLS	*Louis L'Amour* 40p
☐ 08157 4	FALLON	*Louis L'Amour* 40p
☐ 07815 8	MATAGORDA	*Louis L'Amour* 40p

MORGAN KANE

☐ 09425 0	DUEL IN TOMBSTONE No. 23	*Louis Masterson* 35p
☐ 09467 6	TO THE DEATH, SENOR KANE! No. 24	*Louis Masterson* 35p
☐ 09764 0	BLOODY EARTH No. 28	*Louis Masterson* 30p
☐ 09794 2	NEW ORLEANS GAMBLE No. 29	*Louis Masterson* 30p
☐ 09877 9	APACHE BREAKOUT No. 30	*Louis Masterson* 35p

SUDDEN

☐ 08811 0	SUDDEN	*Oliver Strange* 50p
☐ 09117 0	SUDDEN TAKES THE TRAIL	*Oliver Strange* 35p
☐ 09118 9	THE LAW O' THE LARIAT	*Oliver Strange* 35p
☐ 09063 8	SUDDEN – GOLDSEEKER	*Oliver Strange* 35p
☐ 08907 9	SUDDEN – TROUBLESHOOTER	*Frederick H. Christian* 35p
☐ 08813 7	SUDDEN AT BAY	*Frederick H. Christian* 30p

All these books are available at your bookshop or newsagent: or can be ordered direct from the publisher. Just tick the titles you want and fill in the form below.

....

CORGI BOOKS, Cash Sales Department, P.O. Box 11, Falmouth, Cornwall.

Please send cheque or postal order, no currency.
U.K. send 18p for first book plus 8p per copy for each additional book ordered to a maximum charge of 66p to cover the cost of postage and packing.
B.F.P.O. and Eire allow 18p for first book plus 8p per copy for the next 6 books thereafter 3p per book.

NAME (Block letters) ....

ADDRESS ....

(APRIL 76)..

While every effort is made to keep prices low, it is sometimes necessary to increase prices at short notice. Corgi Books reserve the right to show new retail prices on covers which may differ from those previously advertised in the text or elsewhere.